"You're not ready!"

Mark's eyes ran mischievously over Carly's pink bathrobe. "What kind of a reporter are you, Barnett? There's a whole world out there living, dying, loving and fighting. And here you are standing around looking like a giant piece of cotton candy."

Carly retreated a step and cinched her belt tighter. She knew the perils of standing too close to Mark Holbrook while she was wearing a bathrobe. "I'll be ready in ten minutes," she said.

"Make it five," Mark retorted, glancing pointedly at his watch. "We have a plane to catch."

Carly stared at him. "A plane?"

Mark nodded, his hands tucked into his hip pockets. "If we're going to write about fathers' rights, Scoop, you're going to have to do a little research into the subject. We'll start by introducing you to my son."

LINDA
Mixed
LAEL
Messages
MILLER

MIRA BOOKS

ISBN 1-55166-164-0

MIXED MESSAGES

For our Wild Irish Rose,
with love

1

He was a legend, and he was sitting right across the aisle from Carly Barnett. She wondered if she should speak to him and immediately began rehearsing possible scenarios in her mind.

First, she'd sort of bend toward him, then she'd lightly touch his arm. *Excuse me,* she would say, *but I've been following your career since high school and I just wanted to tell you how much I've enjoyed your work. It's partly because of you that I decided to become a journalist.*

Too sappy, she concluded.

She could always look with dismay at the dinner on her fold-down tray and utter, *I beg your pardon, but would you happen to have any Grey Poupon?*

That idea wasn't exactly spectacular, either. Carly hoped she'd be more imaginative once she was working at her new job with Portland's *Oregonian Times.*

Covertly she studied Mark Holbrook as he wrote furiously on a yellow legal pad with his left hand, while ignoring the food the flight attendant had served earlier. He was tall, and younger than Carly would have expected, considering all his accomplishments—he was probably around thirty-two or thirty-three. He had nice brown hair and could have used a shave. Once he glanced at her, revealing expressive brown eyes, but he didn't seem to see Carly at all. He was thinking.

Carly was deflated. After all, she'd been in the limelight herself, though in a very different way from Mr. Holbrook, and men usually noticed her.

She cleared her throat, and instantly his choirboy eyes focused on her.

"Hello," he said with a megawatt smile that made the pit of Carly's stomach jiggle.

She, who was used to being asked things like what she would do if she could run the world for a day, came up with nothing more impressive than, "Hi. Don't you like the food?"

His eyes danced as he lifted the hard roll from his tray and took a deliberate bite.

Carly blushed slightly and thought to herself, *Why didn't I just lean across the aisle and cut his meat for him?*

He had the temerity to laugh at her expression, and that brought the focus of her blue-green eyes back to his face. He was extending his hand. "Mark Holbrook," he said cordially.

Carly had been schooled in deportment all her life, and she couldn't overlook an offered hand. She shook it politely, a little stiffly, and said, "Carly Barnett."

He was squinting at her. "You look sort of familiar. Are you an actress or something?"

Carly relaxed a bit. If she was going to recoil every time someone did something outrageous, she wouldn't last long in the newspaper business. She gave him the smile that had stood her in such good stead during the pageant and afterward. "I was Miss United States four years ago."

"That isn't it," Holbrook replied, dismissing the achievement so briskly that Carly was a little injured. "Have you been in a shaving-cream commercial or something?"

"I don't shave, as a general rule," Carly replied sweetly.

Holbrook chuckled, and it was a nice sound, masculine and easy. "So," he said, "you're a beauty queen."

Carly's smile faded, and she tossed her head in annoyance, making her chin-length blond curls bounce. "I'm a reporter," she corrected him coolly. "Or at least I will be, as of Monday morning."

He nodded. "On TV, of course."

Carly heartily resented the inference that any job she might land would have to hinge on her looks. After all, she'd graduated from college with honors back in Kansas, and she'd even written a weekly column for her hometown newspaper. It wasn't as though she didn't have qualifications. "No," she answered. "I've been hired by the *Oregonian Times*."

Mr. Holbrook's eyes were still dancing, even though his mouth had settled into a circumspect line. "I see. Well, that's one of the best newspapers on the West Coast."

"I know," Carly informed him. "I understand it's a rival to your paper." The instant the words were out of her mouth, she regretted letting on that she knew who he was, but it was too late, so she just sat there, trying to look remote.

Holbrook's grin flashed again. "You're behind on your homework, Ms. Barnett," he informed her. "I went to work for the *Times* two years ago."

They'd be working together, if only for the same paper. While Carly was absorbing that discovery, the flight attendant came and collected their trays, and then they were separated by the beverage cart. When it rolled on by, Carly saw that Mr. Holbrook had an amber-colored drink in one hand.

She felt slightly superior with her tomato juice, but the sensation lasted only until she remembered that Holbrook had a Pulitzer to his credit, that he'd interviewed presidents and kings and some of the greatest movie stars who'd ever graced the silver screen. Because she held him in such high esteem, she was willing to allow for his arrogance.

He'd forgotten all about her, anyway. Now that his dinner tray was out of the way, he was writing on the yellow legal pad in earnest.

The plane began its descent into Portland soon after, and Carly obediently put her tray into the upright position and fastened her seat belt. She was nervous about flying in general and taking off and landing in particular, and she gripped the armrests so tightly that her knuckles ached. Even though she'd flown a lot, Carly had never gotten used to it, and she doubted that she ever would.

When the plane touched down and then bumped and jostled along the runway, moving at a furious pace, Carly closed her eyes tightly and awaited death.

"It's going to be okay," she heard a voice say, and she was startled into opening her eyes again.

Mark Holbrook was watching her with gentle amusement, and he reached across the aisle to grip her hand.

Carly felt foolish, and she forced a shaky smile. But she had to grimace when the engines of the big plane were thrust into reverse and the sound of air rushing past the wings filled the cabin.

"Ladies and gentlemen," a staticky voice said over the sound system, "we'd like to welcome you to Portland, Oregon. There's a light spring rain falling today, and the temperature is in the mid-forties. Thank you for choosing our airline, and we hope you'll fly with us again soon. Please remain in your seats until we've come to a complete stop at the gate..."

Mark was obviously one of those people who never listened to such requests. He released Carly's hand after giving it a squeeze, and stood to rummage through the overhead compartment for his carry-on luggage.

"Need a lift somewhere?" he asked, smiling down at Carly.

For a moment she almost regretted that her friend Janet would be waiting for her inside the terminal. She shook her head. "Thanks, but someone will be picking me up."

He produced a business card from the pocket of his rumpled tweed coat and extended it. "Here," he said with mischief in his eyes. "If you need any help learning the ropes, just call my extension."

She beamed at him and replied in the same teasing tone of voice, "I think I'll be able to master my job on my own, Mr. Holbrook."

He chuckled and moved out of the plane with the rest of the mob, glancing back at Carly once to give her a brazen wink and another knee-dissolving grin.

Ten minutes later, when the crowd had thinned, Carly walked off the plane carrying her beauty case and purse. Her best friend from college, Janet McClain, was waiting eagerly at the gate, as promised.

"I thought you'd missed your flight," Janet fussed as she and Carly hugged. Janet was an attractive brunette with dark eyes, and she'd been working in Portland as a buyer for a major department store ever since graduating from college. She'd been the one to suggest that Carly leave home once and for all and make a life for herself on the coast.

"I didn't want to be in the crush," Carly answered. "Is my apartment ready?"

Janet shook her head. "The paint's still wet, but don't worry about it. You can spend a few days at my place—you need to wait for your furniture to arrive anyway."

Carly nodded. In the distance she caught a glimpse of the back of Mark Holbrook's head. She wished she could see if he was walking with anyone, but even at her height of five feet seven inches the effort was fruitless.

"Who are you staring at?" Janet demanded, sensing drama. "Did you meet somebody on the plane?"

"Sort of," Carly admitted. "I was sitting across the aisle from Mark Holbrook."

Janet looked suitably impressed. "The journalist? What was he doing in coach?"

Carly laughed. "Slumming, I guess."

Janet's cheeks turned pink. "I didn't mean it like that," she said, shoving her hands into the pockets of her raincoat. "Did you actually talk to him?"

"Oh, yes," Carly answered. "He condescended to say a few words."

"Did he ask you out?"

Carly sighed. She wished he had and, at the same time, was glad he hadn't. But she wasn't prepared to admit to such confusion—reporters were supposed to be decisive, with clear-cut opinions on everything. "He gave me his card."

After that, Janet let the subject drop even though, these days, judging by her letters and phone calls, she was fixated on the man-woman relationship. She'd developed a penchant to get married and have a child.

They picked up Carly's luggage and had a porter carry it to Janet's car, which was in a far corner of the parking lot. The May sky glowered overhead.

"Well, Monday's the big day," Janet remarked when they had put Carly's bags in the trunk and Janet's stylish car was jetting sleekly into heavy afternoon traffic. "Are you excited?"

Carly nodded, but she couldn't help thinking of home. It was later there; her dad would be leaving his filling station for the day and going home. Since his daughter wasn't there to look after him, he'd probably buy fast food for supper and drive his cholesterol count sky high.

"You're pretty quiet," Janet observed. "Having second thoughts?"

Carly shook her head resolutely. She'd dreamed of working on a big-city newspaper all her life, and she had no real regrets. "I was just thinking of my dad. With me gone, there's nobody there to take care of him."

"Good grief, Carly," Janet immediately retorted, "you make him sound ancient. How old is he—forty-five?"

Carly sighed. "Fifty. And he doesn't eat right."

Janet tossed her an impish grin. "With his old-maid daughter out of the way, your dad will probably fall madly in love with some sexy widow or divorcée and have a wild affair. Or maybe he'll get married again and father a passel of kids."

Carly grinned and shook her head, but as she looked out at the rain-misted Oregon terrain, her expression turned wistful. Here was her chance to live out her dreams and really be somebody besides a beauty queen.

She hoped she had what it took to succeed in the real world.

Carly's new apartment was in Janet's building, and it was a simple one-bedroom unit painted white throughout. Since the walls were still wet, it smelled of chemical fumes.

The carpets, freshly cleaned, were a toasty beige color, and there was a fireplace, fronted with fake white marble, in the living room. Carly looked forward to reading beside a crackling wood fire in her favorite chenille bathrobe.

"What do you think?" Janet asked, spreading her arms as though she'd conjured the whole place, like a modern-day Merlin.

Carly smiled, wishing the paint were dry and her furniture had arrived. It would have been nice to settle in and start getting used to her new home. "It's great. Thanks for taking the time to find it for me, Janet."

"It wasn't any big deal, considering that I live in this building. Come on, we'll change our clothes, get some supper out and take in a movie."

"You're sure you don't have a date?" Carly asked, following her friend out of the apartment.

They had already taken the suitcases to Janet's place.

"He'll keep," Janet answered with a mysterious smile.

Carly thought of Reggie, her erstwhile fiancé, and wondered what he was doing at that very moment. Making rounds at the hospital, probably. Or swimming at the country club. She seriously doubted that he missed her; his career was the real priority in his life. "Are you in love?"

They were all the way to Janet's door before she answered. "I don't really know. Tom is good-looking and nice, and he has a good job. Maybe those things are enough—maybe love is just a figment of some poet's imagination."

Carly shook her head as she followed her friend into an apartment that was virtually a duplicate of the one they'd just left, except for the carpet. Here, it was forest green. "I wouldn't do anything rash if I were you," she warned. "There might just be something to this love business."

"Yeah," Janet agreed, tossing her purse onto the sofa and shrugging out of her raincoat. "Bruised hearts and insomnia."

After that, Carly stopped trying to win her friend over to her point of view. She didn't know the first thing about love herself, except that she'd never been in it, not even with Reggie.

* * *

"An advice column?" Carly's voice echoed in her cramped corner office the following Monday morning. "But I thought I was going to be a reporter...."

Carly's new boss, Allison Courtney, stood tall and tweedy in the doorway. She was a no-nonsense type, with alert gray eyes, sleek blond hair pulled tightly into a bun and impeccable make-up. "When we hired you, Carly, we thought you were a team player," she scolded cordially.

"Of course I am, but—"

"A lot of people would kill for a job like this, you know. I mean, think of it. You're getting paid to *tell other people what to do,* for heaven's sake!"

Carly had pictured herself interviewing senators and homeless people, covering trials and stand-offs between the police and the underworld. She knew the advice column was a plum, but it had never occurred to her that she'd be asked to serve in that capacity, and she was frankly disappointed. Calling upon years of training, she assumed a cheerful expression. "Where do I start?"

Allison returned Carly's smile, pleased. "Someone will bring you this week's batch of mail. You'll find all the experts you need listed in the Rolodex. Oh, and between letters you might help out with clerical work and such. Welcome aboard." With that, she stepped out, closing the office door behind her.

Carly set the box down on her desk with a *clunk* and sank into her chair. "Clerical work?" she echoed, tossing a glance at the computer system perched at her elbow. "Good grief. Did I come all the way to Oregon just to be a glorified secretary?"

As if in answer, the telephone on her desk buzzed.

"Carly Barnett," she said into the receiver, after pushing four different buttons in order to get the right line.

"Just seeing if it works," replied a bright female voice. "I'm Emmeline Rogers, and I'm sort of your secretary."

Carly felt a little better, until she remembered that she was probably going to spend as much time doing office work as writing. Maybe more. "Hi," she said shyly.

"Want some coffee or something?"

Carly definitely felt better. "Thanks. That would be great."

Moments later, Emmeline appeared with coffee. She was small, with plain brown hair, green eyes and a ready smile. "I brought pink sugar, in case you wanted it."

Carly thanked the woman again and stirred half a packet of sweetener into the hot, strong coffee. "There are supposed to be some letters floating around here somewhere. Do you know where they are?"

Emmeline nodded and then glanced at her watch. Maybe she was one of those people who took an early lunch, Carly thought. "I'll bring them in."

"Great," Carly answered. "Thanks."

Emmeline slipped out and returned five minutes later with a mailbag the size of Santa's sack. In fact, Carly was reminded of the courtroom scene in *Miracle On 34th Street* when the secretary spilled letters all over her desk.

By the time Emmeline had emptied the bag, Carly couldn't even see over the pile. She would have to unearth her computer and telephone before she could start working.

"I couldn't think of a way to break it to you gently," Emmeline said.

Carly took a steadying sip of her coffee and muttered, "Allison said I'd be helping out with clerical work during slack times."

Emmeline smiled. "Allison thinks she has a sense of humor. The rest of us know better."

Carly chuckled and shoved the fingers of her left hand through her hair. Until two weeks ago, when she'd made the final decision to break off with

Reggie and come to Oregon, she'd worn it long. The new cut, reaching just a couple of inches below her earlobes, had been a statement of sorts; she was starting over fresh.

Emmeline left her with a little shrug and a sympathetic smile. "Buzz me if you need anything."

Carly was beginning to sort the letters into stacks. "If there's another avalanche," she responded, "send in a search party."

Her telephone and computer had both reappeared by the time a brisk knock sounded at her office door. Mark poked his head around it before she had time to call out a "Come in" or even wonder why Emmeline hadn't buzzed to announce a visitor.

"Hi," he said, assessing the mountain of letters with barely concealed amusement. He was probably off to interview the governor or some astronaut.

Carly gave him a dour look. "Hi," she responded.

He stepped into the tiny office and closed the door. "Your secretary's on a break," he said. He was wearing jeans, a plaid flannel shirt and a tan corduroy jacket.

"What I need is a moat stocked with crocodiles," Carly retorted with a saucy smile. She wasn't sure how she felt about this man—he produced an odd tangle of reactions that weren't easy to unravel and define. The impact of his presence was almost overwhelming—he seemed to fill the room, leaving no space for her—and Carly was both intrigued and frightened.

She was at once attracted to him, and defensive about her lack of experience as a journalist.

Mark drew up the only extra chair, turned it around backward and sat astraddle of it, resting his arms across the back. "What are they going to call this column now? 'Dear Miss Congeniality'?"

"I wasn't Miss Congeniality," Carly pointed out, arching her eyebrows and deliberately widening her eyes.

"Little wonder," he replied philosophically.

Carly leaned forward in her chair and did her best to glower. "Was there something you wanted?"

"Yes. I'd like you to go to dinner with me tonight."

Carly was putting rubber bands around batches of letters and stacking them on her credenza. A little thrill pirouetted up her spine and then did a triple flip to the pit of her stomach. Even though every instinct she possessed demanded that she refuse, she found herself nodding. "I'd enjoy that."

"We could take in a movie afterward, if you want."

Carly looked at the abundance of letters awaiting her attention. "That would be stretching it. Maybe some other time."

Idly Mark picked up one of the letters and opened it. His handsome brow furrowed as he read. "This one's from a teenage girl," he said, extending the missive to Carly. "What are you going to tell her?"

Carly took the page of lined notebook paper and scanned it. The young lady who'd written it was still in high school, and she was being pressured by the boy she dated to "go all the way." She wanted to know how she could refuse without losing her boyfriend.

"I think she should stand her ground," Carly said. "If the boy really cares about her, he'll understand why she wants to wait."

Mark nodded thoughtfully. "Of course, nobody expects you to reply to every letter," he mused.

Carly sensed disapproval in his tone, though it was well masked. "What's wrong with my answer?" she demanded.

"It's a little simplistic, that's all." His guileless brown eyes revealed no recriminations.

Without understanding why, Carly was on the defensive. "I suppose you could come up with something better?"

He sighed. "No, just more extensive. I would tell her to talk to a counselor at school, or a clergyman, or maybe a doctor. Things are complex as hell out there, Carly. Kids have a lot more to worry about than making cheerleader or getting on the football team."

Carly sat back in her hair and folded her arms. "Could it be, Mr. Holbrook," she began evenly, "that you think I'm shallow just because I was Miss United States?"

He grinned. "Would I have asked you out to dinner if I thought you were shallow?"

"Probably."

Mark shrugged and spread his hands. "I'm sure you mean well," he conceded generously. "You're just inexperienced, that's all."

She took up a packet of envelopes and switched on her computer. The printer beside it hummed efficiently at the flip of another switch. "I won't ever have any experience," she responded, "if you hang around my office for the rest of your life, picking my qualifications apart."

He stood up. "I assume you have a degree in psychology?"

"You know better."

Mark was at the door now, his hand on the knob. "True. I looked you up in the Reader's Digest book of Beauty Queens. You majored in—"

"Journalism," Carly interrupted.

Although his expression was chagrined, his eyes twinkled as he offered her a quick salute. "See you at dinner," he said, and then he was gone.

Thoroughly unsettled, Carly turned her attention back to the letters she was expected to deal with.

Resolutely she opened an envelope, took out the folded page and began to read.

By lunchtime, Carly's head was spinning. She was certainly no Pollyanna, but she'd never dreamed there were so many people out there leading lives of quiet desperation.

Slipping on her raincoat and reaching for her purse and umbrella, she left the *Times* offices and made her way to a cozy little delicatessen on the corner. She ordered chicken salad and a diet cola, then sat down at one of the round metal tables and stared out at the people hurrying past the rain-beaded window.

After a morning spent reading about other people's problems, she was completely depressed. This was a state of mind that just naturally conjured up thoughts of Reggie.

Carly lifted her soft drink and took a sip. Maybe she'd done the wrong thing, breaking her engagement and leaving Kansas to start a whole new life. After all, Reggie was an honest-to-God doctor. He was already making over six figures a year, and he owned his sprawling brick house outright.

Glumly Carly picked up her plastic fork and took a bite of her salad. Perhaps Janet was right, and love *was* about bruised hearts and insomnia. Maybe it was some kind of neurotic compulsion.

Hell, maybe it didn't exist at all.

At the end of her lunch hour, Carly returned to her office to find a note propped against her computer screen. It was written on the back of one of the envelopes, in firm black letters that slanted slightly to the right. *This guy needs professional help. Re: dinner—meet me downstairs in the lobby at seven. Mark.*

Carly shook her head and smiled as she took the letter out of the envelope. Her teeth sunk into her lower lip as she read about the plight of a man who was in love with his Aunt Gertrude. Nothing in journalism school, or in a year's reign as Miss United States, had prepared her for dealing with things like this.

She set the letter aside and opened another one.

Allison popped in at five minutes before five. "Hello," she chimed. "How are things going?"

Carly worked up a smile. "Until today," she replied, "I had real hope for humanity."

Allison gestured toward the Rolodex on the credenza. "I trust you're making good use of Madeline's files. She made some excellent contacts in the professional community while she was here.''

Madeline, of course, was Carly's predecessor, who had left her job to join her professor husband on a sabbatical overseas. "I haven't gotten that far," Carly responded. "I'm still in the sorting process."

Allison shook a finger at Carly, assuming a stance and manner that made her resemble an elementary school librarian. "Now remember, you have deadlines, just like everyone else at this paper."

Carly nodded. She was well aware that she was expected to turn in a column before quitting time on Wednesday. "I'll be ready," she said, and she was relieved when Allison left it at that and disappeared again.

She was stuffing packets of letters into her briefcase when Janet arrived to collect her.

"So how was it?" Janet asked, pushing a button on the elevator panel. The doors whisked shut.

"Grueling," Carly answered, patting her briefcase with the palm of one hand. "Talk about experience. I'm expected to deal with everything from the heartbreak of psoriasis to nuclear war."

Janet smiled. "You'll get the hang of it," she teased. "God did."

Carly rolled her eyes and chuckled. "I think he divided the overflow between Abigail Van Buren, Ann Landers and me."

In the lobby the doors swished open, and Carly found herself face-to-face with Mark Holbrook. Perhaps because she was unprepared for the encounter, she felt as though the floor had just dissolved beneath her feet.

Janet nudged her hard in the ribs.

"M-Mark, this is Janet McClain," Carly stammered with all the social grace of a nervous ninth grader. "We went to high school and college together."

Carly begrudged the grin Mark tossed in Janet's direction. "Hello," he said suavely, and Carly thought, just fleetingly, of Cary Grant.

Mark's warm brown eyes moved to Carly. "Remember—we're supposed to meet at seven for dinner."

Carly was still oddly star struck, and she managed nothing more than a nod in response.

"I take back every jaded remark I've ever made about love," Janet whispered as she and Carly walked away. "I've just become a believer."

Carly was shaken, but for some reason she needed to put on a front. "Take it from me, Janet," she said cynically, "Mark Holbrook may look like a prize, but he's too arrogant to make a good husband."

"Umm," said Janet.

"I mean, it's not like every dinner date has to be marriage material—"

"Of course not," Janet readily agreed.

A brisk and misty wind met them as they stepped out onto the sidewalk in front of the *Times* building, and Carly's cheeks colored in a blush. She averted her eyes. "I know he's the wrong kind of man for me—with all he's accomplished, he must be driven, like Reggie, but—"

"But?" Janet prompted.

"When he asked me out for dinner, I meant to say no," Carly confessed, "but somehow it came out yes."

2

Carly arrived at the *Times* offices at five minutes to seven, wearing an attractive blue crepe de chine jumpsuit she'd borrowed from Janet and feeling guilty about all the unread letters awaiting her at home.

She stepped into the large lobby and looked around. She shouldn't even be there, she thought to herself. When she'd left home, she'd had a plan for her life, and Mark Holbrook, attractive as he might be, wasn't part of it.

An elevator bell chimed, doors swished open, and Mark appeared, as if conjured by her thoughts. He carried a briefcase in one hand and wore the same clothes he'd had on earlier: jeans, a flannel shirt and a corduroy jacket.

"This almost makes me wish I'd worn a tie," he said, his warm brown eyes sweeping over her with admiration. Another of his lightning-charged grins flashed. "Then again, I'm glad I didn't. You look wonderful, Ms. Congeniality."

Carly let the beauty-pageant vernacular slide by. Although she'd had a lot of experience talking to people, she felt strangely shy around Mark. "Thanks," she said.

They walked three blocks to Jake's, an elegantly rustic restaurant-tavern that had been in business since 1892. When they walked in, the bartender called out a good-natured greeting to Mark, who answered with a thumbs-up sign, then proceeded to the reservations desk.

Soon Mark and Carly were seated in a booth on wooden benches, the backs towering over their heads. A waiter promptly brought them menus and greeted Mark by name.

Carly figured he probably brought a variety of women to the restaurant, and was inexplicably annoyed by the thought. She chose a Cajun plate, while Mark ordered a steak.

"Making any progress with the letters?" he asked when they were alone again.

Carly sighed. She'd probably be up until two or three in the morning, wading through them. "Let's put it this way," she answered, "I should be home working."

The wine arrived and Mark tasted the sample the steward poured, then nodded. The claret was poured and the steward walked away, leaving the bottle behind.

Mark lifted his glass and touched it against Carly's. "To workaholics everywhere," he said.

Carly took a sip of her wine and set the glass aside. The word "workaholic" had brought Reggie to mind, and she felt as though he were sitting at the table with them, an unwelcome third. "What's the most important thing in your life?" she asked to distract herself.

The waiter left their salads, then turned and walked away.

"Things don't mean much to me," Mark responded, lifting his fork. "It's people who matter. And the most important person in my life is my son, Nathan."

Even though she certainly wasn't expecting anything to develop between herself and Mark, Carly was jarred by the mention of a child. "You're not married, I hope," she said, practically holding her breath.

"No, I'm divorced, and Nathan lives in California, with his mother," he said. There was, for just an instant, a look of pain in his eyes. This was quickly displaced by a mischievous sparkle. "Would it matter to you—if I were married, I mean?"

Carly speared a cherry tomato somewhat vengefully. "Would it *matter?* Of course it would."

"A lot of women don't care."

"I'm not a lot of women," Carly responded, her tone resolute.

He shrugged one shoulder. "There's a shortage of marriageable men out there, I'm told. Aren't you worried that your biological clock is ticking, and all that?"

"Maybe in ten years I'll be worried. Right now I'm interested in making some kind of life for myself."

"Which you couldn't do in the Midwest?"

"I wanted to do it here," she said.

Mark smiled. "Exactly what kind of life are you picturing?"

Carly was beginning to feel as though she was being interviewed, but she didn't mind. She understood how a reporter's mind worked. "Mainly I want to write for a newspaper—not advice, but articles, like you do. And maybe I'll buy myself a little house and a dog."

"Sounds fulfilling," Mark replied.

There was so little conviction in his voice that Carly peered across the table at him and demanded, "Just what did you mean by that?"

He widened those guileless choirboy eyes of his and sat back on the bench as though he expected the salt shaker to detonate. "I was just thinking—well, it's a shame that so few women want to have babies anymore."

"I didn't say I didn't want to have babies," Carly pointed out. Her voice had risen, and she blushed to see that the people at the nearest table were looking at her. "I *love* babies," she clarified in an angry whisper. "I plan to breast-feed and everything!"

The waiter startled Carly by suddenly appearing at her elbow to deliver dinner, and Mark grinned at her reaction.

She spoke in a peevish hiss. "Let's just get off this topic of conversation, all right?"

"All right," Mark agreed. "Tell me, what made you start entering beauty pageants?"

It wasn't the subject Carly would have chosen, but she could live with it. "Not 'what,'" she replied. "'Who.' It was my mother. She started entering me in contests when I was four and, except for a few years when I was in an awkward stage, she kept it up until I was old enough to go to college."

"And then you won the Miss United States title?"

Carly nodded, smiling slightly as she recalled those exciting days. "You'd have thought Mom was the winner, she was so pleased. She called everybody we knew."

Mark was cutting his steak. "She must miss you a lot."

Carly bent her head, smoothing the napkin in her lap. "She died of cancer a couple of weeks after the pageant."

When Carly lifted a hand back to the table, Mark's was waiting to enfold it. "I'm sorry," he said quietly.

His sympathy brought quick, stinging tears to her eyes. "It could have been worse," Carly managed to say. "Everything happened almost instantaneously. She didn't suffer much."

Mark only nodded, his eyes caressing Carly in a way that eased the pain of remembering.

"How old is Nathan?" she asked, and the words came out a little awkwardly.

Mark's voice was hoarse when he answered. "He's ten," he replied, opening his wallet and taking out a photo.

Nathan Holbrook was handsome, like his father, with brown hair and eyes, and he was dressed in a baseball uniform and was holding a bat, ready to swing.

Carly smiled and handed the picture back. "It must be difficult living so far away from him," she commented.

Mark nodded, and Carly noticed that he averted his eyes for a moment.

"Is something wrong?" she asked softly.

"Nothing I want to trouble you with," Mark responded, putting away his wallet. "Sure you don't want to go take in a movie?"

Carly thought of the pile of letters she had yet to read. She gave her head a regretful shake. "Maybe some other time. Right now I'm under a lot of pressure to show Allison and the powers-that-be that I can handle this job."

They finished their meal, then Mark settled the bill with a credit card. He held her hand as they walked to his car, which was parked in a private lot beneath the newspaper building.

Barely fifteen minutes later, they were in front of Janet's door. Mark bent his head and gave Carly a kiss that, for all its innocuousness, made her nerve endings vibrate.

"Good night," he murmured, while Carly was still trying to get her bearings. A moment after that, he disappeared into the elevator.

"*Well?*" Janet demanded the second Carly let herself into the apartment.

Carly smiled and shook her head. "It was love at first sight," she responded sweetly. "We're getting married tonight, flying to Rio tomorrow and starting our family the day after."

Janet bounded off the couch and followed Carly as she went through the bedroom and stood outside the bathroom door while she exchanged the jumpsuit for an oversize T-shirt. "Details!" she cried. "Give me details!"

Carly came out of the bathroom, carrying the jumpsuit, and hung it back in the closet. "Mark and I are all wrong for each other," she said.

"How do you figure that?"

Turning away from the closet, Carly shrugged. "The guy sends out mixed messages. He's very attractive, but he's bristly, too. And he's got some very old-fashioned ideas about women."

Janet looked disappointed for a moment, then brightened. "If you're not going to see Mark anymore, how about fixing me up with him?"

Carly was surprised at the strong reaction the suggestion produced in her. She marched across Janet's living room, took her briefcase from the breakfast bar and set it down on the Formica-topped table with a thump. "I didn't say I wasn't going to see him again," she said, snapping the catches and pulling out a stack of letters.

After tossing her friend a smug little smile, Janet said good-night and went off to bed. Carly looked with longing at the fold-out sofa, then made herself a cup of tea and set to work.

Although there was no sign of Emmeline when Carly arrived at work the next morning, suppressing almost continuous yawns and hoping the dark circles under her eyes weren't too pronounced, a memo had been taped to her computer screen.

Staff meeting, the message read. *Nine-thirty, conference room.*

Carly glanced at her watch, sat down at her desk and began reading letters again. It was almost a relief when the time came to leave her small office for the meeting.

The long conference room table was encircled by people, and they all seemed to be talking at the same time. An enormous pot of coffee chortled on a table in the corner, and a blue haze of cigarette smoke lapped at the walls like an intangible tide. Carly poured herself a cup of coffee and sat down in the only empty chair in the room, shaking her head when a secretary came by with a box full of assorted pastries.

Through the sea of smoke, she saw Mark sitting directly across from her. He grinned and tilted his head slightly to one side in a way that was vaguely indulgent.

Mixed messages again, Carly thought, responding with a tight little smile.

The managing editor, a slender, white-haired man with the sleeves of his shirt rolled back to his elbows and suspenders holding up his pants, called the meeting to order.

Carly listened intently as he went over the objectives of the newspaper and gave out assignments.

The best one, a piece on crack houses for the Sunday edition, went to Mark, and Carly felt a sting of envy. While he was out in the field, grappling with real life, she would be tucked away in her tiny office, reading letters from the forlorn.

Mark sat back in his chair, not drinking coffee or eating doughnuts or smoking like the others, his eyes fixed on Carly. She was relieved when the meeting finally ended.

"So," boomed Mr. Clark, the managing editor, just as Carly was pushing back her chair to leave, "how do you like writing the advice column?"

Carly glanced uncomfortably at Mark, who had lingered to open a nearby window. *Now's a nice time to think of that,* she reflected to herself, and Mark looked back at her as though she'd spoken aloud.

She remembered Mr. Clark and his affable question. "I haven't actually written anything yet," she answered diplomatically. "I'm still wading through the letters."

Mark was standing beside the table again, his hands resting on the back of a chair. "You're aware, of course," he put in, "that Ms. Barnett doesn't have any real qualifications for that job?"

Carly looked at him in stunned disbelief, and he favored her with a placid grin.

Mr. Clark was watching Carly, but he spoke as though she wasn't there. "Allison seems to think Ms. Barnett can handle the work," he said thoughtfully, and there was just enough uncertainty in his voice to worry the newest member of his staff.

Carly ignored Mark completely. "You won't be sorry for giving me a chance, Mr. Clark," she said.

The older man nodded distractedly and left the conference room. Carly was right behind him, but a sudden grip on her upper arm stopped her.

"Give me a chance to explain," Mark said in a low voice.

The man had done his best to get her fired, and after she'd uprooted herself and spent most of her life savings to move to Oregon, too.

"There's no need for explanations," she told him, wrenching her arm free of his hand. "You've made your opinion of my abilities perfectly clear."

He started to say something in response, then stopped himself and, with an exasperated look on his face, stepped past Carly and disappeared into his office.

She went back to her office and continued working. By noon she'd read all the letters and selected three to answer in her column. The problems were clear-cut, in Carly's opinion, and there was no need to contact any of the experts in Madeline's Rolodex. All a person needed, she thought to herself, was a little common sense.

She was just finishing the initial draft of her first column when there was a light rap at the door and Allison stepped in. She hadn't been at the staff meeting, and she looked harried.

"Is the column done by any chance?" she asked anxiously. "We could really use some help over in Food and Fashion."

Carly pushed the print button on the keyboard and within seconds handed Allison the hard copy of her column.

Allison scanned it, making *hmm* sounds that told Carly exactly nothing, then nodded. "This will do, I guess. I'll take you to F&F and you can help Anthony for the rest of the day. He's at his wit's end."

Carly was excited. She wouldn't be accompanying the police on a crack-house raid like Mark, but she might at least get to cover a fashion show or a bake-off. Either one would get her out of the building.

Anthony Cornelius turned out to be a slim, good-looking young man with blond hair and blue eyes. Allison introduced Carly, then disappeared.

"I've been perishing to meet you," Anthony said with a straight face. "I would have said hello at the staff meeting, but the smoke was absolutely blinding me. I couldn't *wait* to get out of there."

Carly smiled. "I know what you mean," she said as Anthony gestured toward a chair facing his immaculate desk.

"I've got a tape of your pageant, you know. You were splendid."

"Thank you," Carly demurred. She was getting a little embarrassed at the reminders of past glories.

Anthony gave a showy sigh. "Well, enough chitchat. I'm just *buried* in work, and I'm desperate for your help. There's a cooking contest at the St. Regis Hotel today, while the mall is putting on the biggest fashion show *ever*. Needless to say, I can't be in two places at once."

Carly hid her delight by crossing her legs and smoothing her light woolen skirt. "What would you like me to do?"

"You may have your choice," Anthony answered, frowning as he flipped through a notebook on his desk. "Fashion or food."

Carly had already thought the choice through. "I'll take the cooking contest," she said.

"Fabulous," Anthony responded without looking up from his notes. "St. Regis Hotel, two-fifteen. I've already sent a photographer over. I'll see you back here afterward."

Eagerly Carly rose from her chair and headed for the door. "Anthony?"

He raised his eyes inquiringly.

"Thanks," Carly said, and then she hurried out.

After collecting her purse, notebook and coat, Carly set off for the St. Regis Hotel, which turned out to be within walking distance of the newspaper office. She spent several happy hours interviewing amateur chefs and tasting their special dishes, and she even managed to get them to divulge a few secret recipes.

Returning to her office late that afternoon, having forgotten lunch entirely, Carly absorbed the fact that a new batch of letters had been delivered and sat down at her computer to write up the piece on the cooking contest.

Anthony turned out to be a taskmaster, despite his gentle ways, and Carly willing did three rewrites before he was satisfied. She was about to switch off her computer and go home for the day, taking a briefcase full of letters with her, when a message appeared unbidden on the screen.

"Hello, Carly," it read.

Frowning, Carly pushed her big reading glasses up the bridge of her nose and typed the response without thinking. "Hello."

"How about having dinner with me again tonight? I'll cook."

It was Mark. She wondered whether the message was appearing on every computer screen in the office, or just hers. In the end it didn't matter, since it was late and most everyone else had already gone home. "No, thanks," she typed resolutely. "I never dine with traitors."

"I'll explain if you'll just give me the chance."

"How are you doing this?"

"Trade secret. Do we have a date or not?"

"No."

"Will begging help?"

Carly shut off her computer, filled her briefcase with letters and left the office. She walked to the department store where Janet was employed and found that her friend was still working.

After consulting a schedule, Carly caught a bus back to the apartment building and was overjoyed when the manager, Mrs. Pickering, greeted her with the news that her car and furniture had been delivered.

"I made sure they set up the bed for you," the plump, middle-aged woman said as Carly turned the key in the lock.

The living room was filled with boxes, but the familiar couch and chair were there, as was the small television set. The dining table was in its place next to the kitchenette.

Carly set her briefcase and purse down on the small desk in the living room, then lifted the receiver on her telephone. She heard a dial tone and smiled. Her service was connected.

Feeling unaccountably domestic, Carly thanked Mrs. Pickering for her trouble and set out immediately for the parking lot. Her blue Mustang, one of the prizes she'd won as Miss United States, was in its proper slot.

Taking the keys from her purse, Carly unlocked the car, got behind the wheel and started the engine. She drove to the nearest all-night supermarket and bought a cartful of food and cleaning supplies, then came home and made herself a light supper of soup and salad in her own kitchen.

She dialed Janet's number and left a message on her friend's answering machine, then called her father, knowing he'd be up watching the news.

Don Barnett picked up the telephone on the second ring and gave his customary gruff hello.

"Hi, Dad. It's Carly."

She heard pleasure in his voice. "Hello, beautiful," he said. "All settled in?"

Carly sat down in her desk chair and told her father all about her apartment and her new job.

He listened with genuine interest, and then announced that Reggie was engaged to a nurse from Topeka.

"It didn't take him long, did it?" Carly asked. She wasn't sure what she'd expected—maybe that Reggie would at least have the decency to pine for a month or two.

Her father chuckled. "Having a few second thoughts, are you?"

"No," Carly said honestly. "I just didn't think I was quite so forgettable, that's all." They talked a little longer, then ended the call with promises to stay in touch.

Carly was feeling homesick when a knock sounded at her door. She had never been very close to her mother, despite the inordinate amount of time they'd spent together, but her dad was a kindred spirit.

She put one eye to the peephole and sighed when she saw Mark standing in the hallway.

She opened the door to the length of the chain and looked out at him uncharitably. "Aren't you supposed to be participating in a crack-house raid or something?"

He flashed one of his lethal grins. "That's tomorrow night. May I come in?"

The living room was still filled with unopened boxes, and Carly was wearing her pink bathrobe. Her hair was probably a mess, too. And this man had tried to get her fired just that morning.

Despite all these things, Carly unfastened the chain and opened the door.

Mark was wearing jeans and a navy-blue football jersey with the number "39" printed on it in white, and he carried a bouquet of pink daisies.

Carly eyed them with a certain disdain, even though she secretly loved daisies. "If you think a few flowers are going to make up for the way you sandbagged me this morning—"

Mark sighed. "I was trying to get Clark to move you to another assignment."

"I'll be lucky if you didn't get me booted out instead," Carly replied. Grudgingly she took the daisies, carried them to the kitchenette and filled a glass with water.

When she turned around, she collided with Mark, and, for several excruciatingly sweet moments, her body seemed to be fused to his. She was possessed by a frightening and completely unexpected urge to bare herself to him, to feel his flesh against hers.

She shook her head as if to awaken herself from a dream and started to step around him.

He pinned her against the counter, using just his hips, and Carly felt heat rise from her stomach to her face as he took the daisies and set them aside. His voice was a low, rhythmic rumble.

"I'm not through apologizing," he said, and then he bent his head and touched Carly's lips tentatively with his own.

She gave a little whimper, because she wanted so much to spurn him and could not, and the kiss deepened. He shaped her mouth with his, and explored its depths with his tongue.

Even with Reggie, the man she'd planned to marry, Carly had been able to withstand temptation easily. With Mark, things were startlingly different. He had overridden her resistance, stirring a sudden and brutal need within her with a simple kiss.

Carly found herself melting against her kitchen counter like a candle set close to a fire. She had a dizzy, disoriented feeling, as though she'd just stepped off some wild ride at a carnival.

With a little chuckle, Mark withdrew from her mouth only to nibble lightly at the length of her neck. He cupped her breast with his hand, and beneath the terry cloth her nipple pulsed to attention.

She moaned helplessly, and Mark lifted her onto the counter. Then he uncovered the breast he had aroused and began to suck gently on its peak.

Carly drew in a swift breath. She knew she should push him away, but she couldn't quite bring herself to do that. What he was doing felt entirely too good.

He traced her collarbone with kisses and then bared her other breast and took its pink tip boldly into his mouth.

Carly gave a strangled groan and let her head fall back against the cupboard door. With one of her hands, she clutched Mark's shoulder, and with the other she pressed the back of his head, holding him close to her.

She clasped his waist between her knees, as though to keep from flying away, and when she felt his hand move down over her belly, she could only tremble. When he found her secret, and began to caress it with his fingers, she started and cried out softly.

"Shh," he said against her moist, well-suckled nipple. "It's all right."

Carly, who had never given herself to a man before, sought his lips with her own, desperate for his kiss. He mastered her mouth thoroughly, then went back to her breasts. He continued his gentle plundering, and Carly's heels rose to the counter's edge in a motion of abject surrender.

Mark kissed his way down her belly and wrung a raw gasp from her throat when he took her boldly into his mouth. He gripped Carly's ankles firmly, parting her legs until she was totally vulnerable to him.

A fine sheen of perspiration covered her body as he attended her, and her hair clung, moist, to her forehead and her cheeks. She writhed and twisted, murmuring nonsense words, while Mark drove her toward sweet damnation.

She cried out at the fiery tumult shuddering through her body, surrendered shamelessly to the searing pleasure. And when it was over, tears of confusion and relief trickled down her cheek.

Gently Mark released her ankles so that she could lower her legs. He closed her robe and kissed her damp brow softly.

"Oh, God," Carly whispered, as shame flowed into her, like water rushing into a tide pool.

Mark traced her lips with the tip of one finger, and considered her with kind eyes. "Chemistry," he said, and then, to Carly's utter amazement, he turned away.

She scooted off the counter and stood for several moments, waiting for her knees to stabilize. Mark had already reached the door, and his hand was resting on the knob.

Carly cinched the belt of her bathrobe tightly. She couldn't believe it. This man had aroused her thoroughly, had subjected her to a scorching climax—and now he was *leaving*. "Where are you going?"

The insolent brown eyes caressed her as he opened the door. "Home."

"But..."

There was a touch of sadness to his smile. "Yes," he said, answering her unspoken question, "I want you. But we're going to wait."

Carly was finally able to move. She stumbled a few steps toward him, filled with resentment because he'd made her need him so desperately and then dismissed her. "You would have been the first," she taunted him, her voice barely above a whisper.

His eyes slid over her slender body, which was still quivering with outrage and violent appeasement. "I'll be the first," he assured her, "and the last."

And then he was gone.

3

Carly didn't see Mark the next day, but another mysterious message appeared on her computer screen late in the afternoon, just as she was getting ready to go home.

"Nice coverage on the food contest," the glowing green letters said, "but telling 'Frazzled in Farleyville' to get a divorce was truly cavalier. Who the hell do you think you are, Joyce Brothers?"

Carly sighed. All her life, her view of the world had been pretty clear-cut: this was right, that was wrong; this was good, that was bad. Now she was faced with a man who could melt her bones one moment, and attack her most basic principles the next.

She poised her fingers over the keyboard for a few minutes, sinking her teeth into her lower lip, then typed, "If you don't like my column, Holbrook, do us both a favor and stop reading it."

Mark's response took only seconds to appear. "That's what I like," it jibed. "A rookie who knows how to heed the voice of experience."

"Thank you, Ann Landers," Carly typed succinctly. "Good night, and goodbye." With that, she shut down the system, gathered up her things and left the room.

Somewhat to her disappointment, there were no computer messages from Mark the next day or the one after that, and he didn't appear in any of the staff meetings, either.

Carly told herself she was relieved, but she was also concerned. She worried, at odd moments, about Mark's undercover assignment with the police. A thousand times a day she wondered how soon word would leak out if something went wrong...

A full week had passed when she encountered Mark again, at a media party in the ballroom of a downtown hotel. He was wearing jeans, a lightweight blue sweater and a tweed sports jacket while all the other men sported suits, and he still managed to look quietly terrific.

His eyes flipped over Carly's slinky pink sheath, and instantly her nipples hardened and pressed against the glimmering cloth. "Hi," he said, and the word was somehow intimate, bringing back

Technicolor memories of the incident on her kitchen counter.

Carly's cheeks went as pink as her dress, and she folded her arms in self-defense. "Well," she said acidly, "I see you survived the crack raid."

Mark took hold of her elbow and gently but firmly escorted her through the crush of television, radio and newspaper people toward the lobby. "We need to talk."

Carly glared at him. "I think it would be best if we just communicated through our computers. Better yet," she added, starting to move around him, "let's not communicate at all."

He captured her arm again, pulled her back and pressed her to sit on a bench upholstered in royal-blue velvet. He took a seat beside her and looked into her eyes, frowning. "What did I do now?"

She straightened her spine, drew a deep breath and let it out again. "That has to be the most obtuse question I've ever heard," she said stiffly.

"I doubt it," Mark retorted, before she could go on to say that she didn't appreciate his criticism and his nonchalant efforts to get her fired. "Considering that you've probably been asked things like, 'How do you walk without your tiara falling off?' and 'What contribution do you think tap dancing will make to world peace?' "

Carly leaned close to him and spoke through her teeth. "I'd appreciate it, Mr. Hotshot Pulitzer Prize Winner, if you would stop making comments about my title!"

His wonderful, damnable brown eyes twinkled. "Okay," he conceded, "just answer one question, and I will."

Carly was cautious. "Fair enough," she allowed huffily. "Ask away."

"What was your talent?"

"I beg your pardon?"

"In the pageant. When the other semifinalists sang and danced and played stirring classical pieces on the piano, what did you do?"

Carly swallowed and averted her eyes.

Mark prompted her with a little nudge.

"I twirled a baton," she blurted out in a furious whisper. "Are you satisfied?"

"No," Mark replied, and even though he wasn't smiling, his amusement showed in every line of his body. "But I'll let the subject drop for the time being."

"Good," Carly growled, and sprang off the bench.

Mark pulled her back down again. "Lighten up, Barnett," he said. "If you can't take a little ribbing, you won't last five minutes in this business."

Carly's face was flushed, and she yearned to get out into the cool, crisp May evening. "So now I'm thin-skinned, as well as incompetent."

He chuckled and shook his head. "I never said you were incompetent, but you're damned cranky. I can't figure out which you need more—a good spanking or a very thorough session on a mattress."

That was it. Carly had reached the limit of her patience. She jumped up off the bench again and stormed back into the party.

She would have preferred to walk out of that hotel, get into her car and drive home. But she knew contacts were vital, and she wanted to meet as many people as she could.

She stayed an hour and a half, avoiding Mark, passing out and collecting business cards. Then she put on her shiny white taffeta blazer and headed for the parking lot.

She had unlocked the door and slid behind the wheel before she realized that Mark was sitting in the passenger seat. Surprise and fury made her gasp. "How did you get in here? This car was locked!"

He grinned at her. "I learned the trick from Iggy DeFazzio, a kid I interviewed when I was doing a piece on street gangs."

Carly knew it wouldn't do any good to demand that he leave her car, and she wasn't strong enough to throw him out bodily. She started the ignition and glared at him. "Where to, Mr. Holbrook?"

"My place," he said with absolute confidence that he'd get his way.

"Has anybody ever told you that you are totally obnoxious?"

"No, but my teenage niece once said I was totally awesome, and I think she meant it as a compliment."

Carly pulled out into the light evening traffic. "You must have paid her."

Mark spoke pleasantly. "Pull over."

"Why?"

"Because I can't grovel and give directions at the same time," he replied.

Wondering why she was obeying when this man had done nothing but insult her since the moment she'd met him, Carly nonetheless stopped the car and surrendered the wheel to Mark. Soon they were speeding down the freeway.

"So," he began again brightly, "when you were twirling your baton, were the ends on fire?"

Carly reached out and slugged him in the arm, but a grin tugged at the corners of her mouth. "Is this your idea of groveling?"

He laughed. "Meet anybody interesting at the party?"

"Two or three TV newscasters and a talk-show host," she answered, watching him out of the corner of her eye. "I'm having dinner with Jim Benson from Channel 37 Friday night."

Mark's jaw tightened for just a moment, and he tossed a sidelong glance in her direction. "He's a lech," he said.

"If he gets out of line," she replied immediately, "I'll just hit him with my baton."

Mark cleared his throat and steered the car onto an exit. "Carly—"

"What?"

"We got off on the wrong foot, you and I."

Carly folded her arms. "Whose fault was that?"

He let out a ragged sigh as they came to a stop at a red light. "For purposes of expediency," he muttered, "I'll admit that it was mine. Partly."

"That's generous of you."

The light changed, and they drove up a steep hill. "Damn it," Mark bit out, "will you just let me finish?"

Carly spread her hands in a motion of generosity. "Go ahead."

He turned onto a long, curving driveway, the headlights sweeping over evergreen trees, giant ferns and assorted brush. "I have a lot of respect for you as a person."

"I haven't heard that one since the night of the junior prom when Johnny Shupe wanted to put his hand down the front of my dress."

The car jerked to a stop beside a compact pickup truck, and Mark shut off the ignition and the headlights. "I get it," he snapped. "You're mad because I only took you part of the way!"

Carly wanted to slap him for bringing up the kitchen-counter incident, even indirectly, but she restrained herself. "Why, you arrogant bastard!" she breathed instead, clenching her fists. "How dare you talk to me like that?"

He got out of the car, slammed the door and came around to her side. Before she thought to push down the lock, he was bending over her, his lips only a whisper away from hers. "This is how," he replied, and then he kissed her.

At first, Carly resisted, stiffening her body and pressing her lips together in a tight line. But soon Mark's persuasive tongue conquered her, and she whimpered with unwilling pleasure, sagging limply against the back of the car seat.

Presently he took her arm and ushered her out of the car and into the house. By the faint glow of the porch light, Carly could see that it was an old-fashioned brick cottage, with wooden shutters on the windows and a fanlight over the door.

In the small entryway he kissed her again, and the sensations the contact stirred in her pushed all thoughts of their differences to the back of her mind.

"It looks like there's one thing we're going to have to get out of our way before we can make sense of what's happening to us, Carly," he said when the kiss was over. He smoothed away her blazer with gentle hands.

Carly, who had been an avowed ice maiden in high school and college, was suddenly as pliant and willing as a sixteenth-century tavern wench. Her body seemed to be waging some kind of heated rebellion against the resolutions of her mind.

She knew she should get into her car and go home, but she couldn't make herself walk away from Mark.

He led her into a pleasantly cluttered living room where lamps were burning and seated her on the couch. Carly watched as he lit a fire on the hearth, then shifted her gaze to a desk facing a bank of windows. A computer screen glowed companionably among stacks of books and papers.

"I do a lot of my work at home," Mark explained, dusting his hands together as he rose from the hearth. "You can't see it now, of course, but there's a great view of the river from those windows."

Carly was still trying to shore up her sagging defenses, but the attempt was largely hopeless. Mark's kisses had left her feeling as though she'd been drugged.

He left the room briefly and returned with two bottles of wine cooler and a couple of glasses. Taking a seat beside Carly on the cushiony sofa, which was upholstered in mauve suede, he opened the bottles and poured.

Carly figured she had about as much chance coming out of this with her virginity intact as she would have escaping a sheik's harem. The crazy thing was, she didn't want to leave.

Mark handed her a glass, and she took a cautious sip.

"I'm really very bright, you know," she said, feeling defensive. "I got terrific grades in college."

He smiled, set his goblet on the coffee table and swung her legs up onto his lap. "Umm-hmm," he said, slipping off her high-heeled shoes one by one and tossing them away.

Some last vestige of pride made Carly stiffen. "You don't believe me!"

Mark ran a soothing hand over her right foot and ankle, and against her will she relaxed again. "I'd be a fool if I didn't," he answered quietly. "There were over a hundred applicants for your job at the *Times*, and all of them were qualified.''

Carly was pleased. ''Really?''

Mark took advantage of the sexy slit on the side of her pink dress to caress the back of her knee. ''Really,'' he said.

She put her glass aside, feeling as though she'd already consumed a reservoir full of alcohol. On the hearth the fire crackled and snapped. ''I really should go straight home,'' she said.

''I know,'' Mark agreed.

''I mean, it's possible that I don't even *like* you.''

''I know that, too,'' he responded with a grin.

''But we're going to make love, aren't we?''

Mark nodded. ''Yes,'' he said, and then he stood and drew Carly off the couch and into a gentle embrace. He kissed her lightly on the tip of the nose. ''If you really want to go home,'' he said, ''it's OK.''

Carly let her forehead rest against his chest and slid her arms around his waist. ''God help me,'' she whispered, ''I want to stay.''

He put a finger under her chin and tilted her head back so he could look into her eyes. He moved his lips as though he meant to speak, but in the end he kissed her instead.

Again, she had the sensation of being swept into some kind of vortex, where none of the usual rules applied. When Mark lifted her into his arms, she laid her head against his shoulder.

He carried her up a set of stairs, along a hallway and into a room so large that Carly was sure it must run the entire length of the house. She noticed a fireplace, the shadowy shapes of chairs and, finally, the huge bed.

Made of dark wood, it stood on a U-shaped ledge, dominating the room. It was a place where a knight might have deflowered his lady, and Carly was filled with a sense of rightness, as well as desire.

Mark carried her up three carpeted steps and set her on her feet. She stood still as he unfastened the back of her dress and then lowered it to her hips.

The moonlight flowing in through the long windows that lined the opposite wall gave Carly's skin the translucent, pearly glow of white opals, and she felt beautiful as Mark stepped back to admire her. His eyes seemed to smolder in the dim light of the room.

After a while, he bent to kiss the pulse point at the base of her throat, and Carly trembled. She felt as though she'd been created for this moment, as though she'd worked toward it through not just one lifetime, but a thousand.

"Mark," she whispered, and that one word held all her confusion, all her wanting.

In slow, methodical motions, he took away her slip and bra and panty hose and laid her, naked, on the velvet spread that covered his bed. "So beautiful," he said hoarsely, and Carly raised her hands over her head in unconscious surrender as she watched him shed his clothes in the shadows.

"I've never—"

He interrupted her with a soft, reassuring kiss. "I know, sweetheart," he said. "I'll be as gentle as I can." And then he lay on his side on the mattress, caressing her breast with his strong hand, toying with the straining nipple, tracing the lines of her waist and hip.

"Mark," Carly moaned. He had kindled a blaze within her that night in her apartment, and now it burned so hot that it threatened to consume her.

He bent to suckle at her breast, and she whimpered in welcome, entangling her fingers in his rich, glossy hair. He allowed her to fondle him for a time, then caught both her wrists in his hand and lifted them above her head again, making her deliciously vulnerable.

With his other hand he made a light, fiery circle on her belly, sweeping lower with each pass until he'd breached the tangle of silk and found the core of her womanhood.

Carly's flesh pulsed against his palm as he made slow, steady rounds, and she felt herself grow moist in response. She arched her neck, her breath coming in shallow gasps, and instinctively spread her legs.

And still Mark suckled her breasts, first one and then the other. Her nipples were taut and wet from his tongue, and she was sure she would die if he didn't satisfy her.

She began to plead, and he left her breasts to position himself between her thighs. As he had once before, he clasped her ankles and set her feet wide of her body, holding them firmly in place.

By the time he burrowed through to take her into his mouth, the rest of her body was as moist as her hard, jutting nipples. She pressed her heels deep into the mattress and gave a lusty cry as he feasted on her womanhood, and her hips writhed in concert with the teasing parries of his tongue that came later.

She flung her hands wildly, first clawing at the bedspread, then gripping his shoulders, then delving into his hair. The short tendrils around her face were dewy, clinging to her forehead and her cheeks as she strained for the relief only nature could provide.

Passion racked her violently, and her body quivered as she thrust it upward to meet the teasing strokes of Mark's tongue. "Finish me," she pleaded without breath. "Oh—Mark—*finish me!*"

He complied fiercely and wrung a sobbing shout from her, cupping his hands under her bottom, holding her high, supporting her until the storm raging inside her body subsided. When the tempest had ceased, he lowered her gently to the mattress, where she lay trembling and filled with wonder.

"Mark," she wept.

Slowly he kissed her moist forehead, her eyelids, her cheeks. He drank from her breasts again, sleepily at first, and then with growing thirst. When he mounted Carly, parting her legs first with a motion of one knee, she welcomed him, though she knew he was about to change her forever.

She moved her hands up and down his muscle-corded back while he drew at her nipple and, finally, she could wait no more.

She clasped his buttocks in her hands and pressed him to her, and he submitted with a groan.

His entry was slow and careful, and every inch he gave Carly only made her want more. There was a brief, tearing pain as he passed the barrier that had sealed her depths to all but him, but in some strange way it made the pleasure keener.

Moaning when he was inside her to the hilt of his manhood, Mark dragged the pillows down from the head of the bed and stuffed them under her so that she was raised to him, in perfect alignment for pleasure.

His second thrust was gentle, but when she urged him with soft, fiery words, he delved deeper.

Carly encircled his waist with her legs and clenched as if to crush him, and the coupling became a tender battle. Near the end, when they were both wild with need and trembling with exhaustion, he caught hold of her hands and thrust them high above her head. While she cursed him with words of love, he held himself still inside her for a long moment, then made a final lunge.

Carly flung back her head and gave a low, guttural wail as her body spasmed around him. He answered with a shout of amazed ecstasy and filled her with his warmth.

They lay like stone for a long time, neither able to speak or move, and then Mark got up from the bed and lifted a still-befuddled Carly into his arms. He carried her into the bathroom and set her, dazed, on the edge of a deep marble tub.

His body was lean and agile as he adjusted the spigots and fetched two enormous white towels from a shelf. He set them close at hand, then eased Carly gently into the water. When it reached a certain depth, he flipped a switch, and powerful jets made the warmth swirl and bubble around her.

Mark turned off the faucets, then got into the tub behind Carly, his powerful legs making a boundary for hers, his arms resting lightly around her waist. He bent to kiss her bare shoulder.

She tilted her head back and looked up at him, only then able to speak. "If I'd known it felt that good, I'd have been promiscuous," she said.

Mark laughed and then nibbled at her nape. "Me, too," he said, and that made Carly twist to look up at him, a broad smile on her face.

"Come on," she said. "You're not going to tell me that was your first time. Even I'm not *that* naive."

He shook his head, and his wonderful eyes were sparkling at her naïveté. "No, babe—you were the only virgin in attendance. But I can honestly say I've never felt exactly that way before."

Carly settled deeper into the water, leaning back against his hairy chest. "I bet you say that to everybody."

He chuckled and moved his lips against the back of her head. "Wrong again," he replied, and then he dipped a hand into the swirling, soothing water and bathed Carly's breasts, one by one.

It was another beginning.

Soon he was caressing her, and she was surrendering, wanting to melt into him again.

When she had to confront him with her need or perish from it, she shifted so that she was facing him and kneeling between his legs.

"You like being in charge, don't you?" she crooned, taking a fresh bar of soap from a brass dish, dipping it into the water, turning it between her hands until they were slick with suds.

Mark leaned back, resting his head on the edge of the tub, and grinned insolently. "You didn't seem to mind it a little while ago. In fact, my guess would be that it beat twirling a flaming baton all to hell."

Slowly, sensuously, she began to lather his broad chest, making soapy swirls in the spun sugar down that covered it, teasing his nipples with a mischievous fingertip. "There must be some symbolism in that," she conceded huskily. "But I don't quite see it."

He tilted his head even farther back and closed his eyes with an animal sigh of contentment, and it struck Carly that even surrender required a kind of confidence.

"Think, Barnett," he teased. "Think."

Carly didn't want to think. She wanted to bathe this man, and then turn him inside out, just as he'd done to her. And because of the things he'd taught her, she had a pretty good idea how to go about it.

She took her time washing him, and he submitted, but then he claimed the soap and everything was turned around. Soon every inch of Carly was scrubbed to a delicate ivory pink, and she was limp as the cloth Mark had used to cleanse her.

He got out of the tub, lifting her after him, and flipped off the jets under the water. Then he pulled the plug and wrapped one of the huge towels around Carly like a sling, using it to draw her close to him.

She felt his staff rising hard and insistent between them.

"Oh, Mark," she whispered sleepily, "I can't— not again."

"That's what you think," he replied, his lips against her forehead. And he took her back to his bed, where he dried her and laid her out on the sheet like a delicacy to be enjoyed at leisure.

He joined her beneath the covers, knelt between her legs so she couldn't close them to him, and slid his hands under her bottom to lift her to his mouth.

"I mean it," she whimpered as he placed her legs over his shoulders. "I can't—"

He disciplined her with a few flicks of his tongue, and she moaned as heat surged through her tired body, giving it new life.

Mark chuckled against her hardening flesh. "That's what I thought," he said, and he held her firmly in place while she rode helplessly on his lips, her head twisting from side to side in delirium.

He was ruthless. Carly was drenched with perspiration within minutes, and she locked her heels behind his head when he brought her to climax.

After that she begged him to take her and then let her sleep, but he wouldn't. He put her in a new position and made her perform again, and he granted her no quarter until the last shuddering tremor had been drawn from her and her cries of pleasure had died away in the darkness.

Finally she gathered the strength to take revenge. She fell to him, like a starving woman would fall to food, and began to consume him.

At last, Carly had found the way to prevail in the age-old war of lovers, and she was no more merciful to Mark than he had been to her. He groaned like a man in fever, and the sound aroused Carly as much as his caresses and kisses had.

When he could bear no more, he lifted her head and held it from him, gasping as he struggled to catch his breath. Then, ever so gently, he pressed Carly back onto the mattress and took her in a long, slow stroke.

Because his pleasure had excited her so much, she immediately began to convulse, the lower part of her body buckling wildly as he made love to her. Through a sleepy haze she heard him rasp her name, and she felt him stiffen upon her in final release. Then they both were still, and the night rolled in like folds of black velvet and claimed them.

In the morning Carly awakened to the sound of a man whistling. Her aquamarine eyes flew open in alarmed chagrin as she remembered where she was and how she'd behaved in Mark Holbrook's arms.

She sunk her teeth into her lower lip. It was morning, and she was going to have to go home in her slinky pink evening dress.

Just then Mark came out of the bathroom. He was wearing a towel around his hips and there was a toothbrush jutting out of his mouth. He gave Carly a foamy grin, opened a drawer, took out a striped pajama top and tossed it to her.

She scrambled into it, using the blankets to hide behind, and he laughed and went back into the bathroom.

Carly needed a shower, but she wasn't about to pass Mark to get one. Knowing a house that large must have at least one more bath, she hurried out of the room. She found what she sought at the opposite end of the hall and, after locking the door, stepped hastily under a spray of hot water.

When she was clean, she put on the bra, panty hose and slip she'd worn the night before. She was about to shimmy into the dress when a knock sounded at the door.

"It's early, Carly," Mark said cheerfully, as though this were a perfectly ordinary morning. "I'll go over to your apartment and get your things if you'll give me the key."

She pressed her cheek to the door panel, embarrassed to be sending a man for such personal items as clothes and underwear and makeup, but she named off the things she wanted. When she was sure he was gone, she stepped out into the hallway, only to find Mark leaning against the opposite wall, grinning at her.

He moved his gaze slowly, possessively, over her figure. "Like I said," he told her in a voice that was as effective as a kiss or a caress, "it's early."

4

Carly dodged back into the bathroom and slammed the door, and Mark responded with a laugh.

"Regrets?" he asked.

"Yes!" Carly shouted back. She shoved both hands through her hair. "Go away and leave me alone."

"Cranky," he observed in a resigned tone. "Maybe I should have tried the spanking."

Carly turned the lock, then went to the sink and started the water running full blast. She hummed loudly to let Mark know she wasn't paying any attention to anything he was saying—if he was saying anything.

Fifteen minutes had passed before she dared peer into the hallway again.

Mark was gone then—the house seemed to echo with his absence—and Carly put his pajama top on over her underthings and stepped out of the bathroom.

On her way to the kitchen, where she hoped to find coffee perking, Carly passed through the living room. Once again the computer caught her eye. Since Mark wasn't around to see, she ventured over to the desk, sat down in the chair and squinted at the words on the screen.

Excitement brought her to the edge of the chair as she read backward through what was apparently a stage play. The story centered around the painful demise of a marriage, and it was so gripping that Carly forgot her quest for coffee, rummaged through her purse for her glasses and read on.

She didn't stop until she heard a car door slam in the driveway. The sound brought her back to the present with a jerk, and it suddenly occurred to her that Mark might not want her reading his play. Her heart beating double time, she pressed her finger to the "Page Down" key and held it there until the original material was back on the screen.

She was in the kitchen, pouring coffee into a mug, when Mark came in carrying her garment bag and beauty case. He gave her a curious look, and she had the uncomfortable feeling that he was picking up on her guilt.

It's a good thing you're not a spy, Barnett, she thought, reaching out for the things Mark had brought her. "Thanks."

He gave her a light kiss on the forehead. "You're welcome," he answered, and the words had a teasing quality to them.

Carly took another sip of her coffee, then set it aside. If she was going to be at work on time, she'd have to get a move on. "How long have you been up?" she asked idly, remembering that Mark's computer had been on when they came in the night before.

He'd poured coffee for himself, and he grinned at her over the rim of the mug. "A couple of hours. I do some of my best writing before the birds get up."

Carly hesitated in the kitchen doorway. She felt strangely at home in Mark's house and his pajama top, and that was disturbing. "Your piece on the crack-house raid was good," she conceded. The article had had top billing in the Sunday edition, and Carly had marveled as she'd read it.

Mark opened the refrigerator and took out eggs, bacon and a carton of orange juice. "Thanks, Barnett," he said briskly. "I'd love to stand here listening to praise all day, but I've got things to do, and so do you."

Carly felt rebuffed. Until he'd spoken, there had been a certain cautious, morning-after closeness between them. Now there was an impassible force field.

Carly turned around and headed back toward the bathroom.

When she came out, ready to leave for the newspaper office, Mark was at his desk. The play was gone from the screen, replaced by some kind of colorful graph, and he was leaning back in his chair, talking on the telephone.

He dismissed Carly with a wave of his hand—the way he might have done the paperboy or a meter reader—and she was stung. *Apparently,* she thought glumly, *I've served my purpose.*

She gathered up her purse and the clothes she'd worn the night before and went out to get into her car. Her spirits lifted a little when she found a single yellow rosebud lying on the seat.

At the office another mailbag full of letters awaited her, as well as three frantic messages from Janet.

Sipping the cup of coffee Emmeline had brought to her, Carly dialed her friend's work number. A secretary put her right through.

"You didn't come home last night!" Janet said, dispensing with the usual "hello."

Carly smiled, even though there was a heavy place in her heart because she'd given herself to the wrong man. "Are you moonlighting for the FBI these days, or what?"

Janet let out a sigh. "I was just worried, that's all. I mean, you're new in town, and there are some real creeps out there—"

"I'm fine, Janet," Carly insisted moderately, getting out her glasses with one hand and slipping them onto her face. Judging by the bulges in the mailbag sitting on her desk, it was going to be a long day.

"You were with Mark Holbrook!" Janet cried, obviously excited at having solved the mystery.

Carly was annoyed. "Janet—"

"I don't mind telling you, I'm impressed."

"Good. I'd hate to think I wasn't living up to my image," Carly said a little stiffly.

Janet made Carly promise that they'd go out for pizza and salad that night after work, then rang off.

Carly immediately set herself to the task of reading and sorting her mail, and her brow crumpled into a frown as she scanned letter after letter berating her for telling "Frazzled in Farleyville" to get a divorce. It was beginning to seem that the public heartily agreed with Mark's assessment of her advice.

She was still reading and disconsolately munching on Cheeze Crunchies from the vending machine in the lounge, when Mark popped into her office at one forty-five that afternoon.

By then she was really feeling cranky. She'd been writing her column for less than two weeks, and everybody in Portland hated her. "What do you want?" she snapped.

Mark grinned in a way that reawakened some of the perturbing feelings she'd had the night before, when they'd somehow gotten past their many differences and visited a new part of the universe. "I came to see if you'd like to go out for lunch, then maybe take in a matinee or something."

Carly took a sip of diet cola and set the can down with a solid thump. "Some of us can't come and go as we please," she replied, glaring at him through the big lenses of her reading glasses. "*Or* take off to a movie in the middle of a workday."

He drew up a chair and sat down with a philosophical sigh. "My older sister is like you. When she gets overtired, and doesn't eat right—" he paused and nodded toward the Cheeze Crunchies "—her blood sugar drops and she takes on the personality of a third-world leader. It's not a pretty sight."

Carly took off her glasses, tossed them aside and rubbed her eyes wearily. "Don't you have to work or something?"

"I'm between assignments," he answered.

The intercom on Carly's desk buzzed, and she pushed the button and said, "Yes?"

"There's a lady psychologist on the phone," Emmeline announced, "and she's hopping mad because you told 'Frazzled in Farleyville'—"

"To get a divorce," Carly finished with a sigh. Her head was pounding. "Put her on," she added with resignation, pushing another button so Mark wouldn't be able to overhear the psychologist's side of the conversation.

He leaned forward to help himself to a Cheeze Crunchy. "It's gonna be a bloodbath," he said, and settled back to watch.

Carly narrowed her eyes at him, then spun her chair around so that her back was turned.

The psychologist introduced herself and proceeded to tell Carly off. "In essence, *Miss* Barnett," the woman finished, "you should be demoted to a position where you can't possibly do any more harm!"

Calling on all her poise-under-pressure training, Carly replied that she was sorry if she'd offended anyone and hung up. When she turned her chair around again, Mark was gone, and the discovery gave her an empty feeling.

Half an hour later she was called into the managing editor's office.

Fully expecting to be fired, to have to go home to her dad in utter disgrace, Carly obeyed the summons, never letting any of her insecurities show.

"We've had some complaints about the way you're handling the advice column," Mr. Clark said when Carly was seated in a chair facing his imposing desk. His expression was sober, and she resisted an urge to bite her lower lip.

She waited in dignified silence.

A smile broke across the editor's face. "And that's good," he boomed. "Means they're reading you. You're shaking them up, jolting them out of their complacency. Which is not to say you couldn't be a little more careful."

Carly's relief was overwhelming. "I'll be sure to check with an expert on the trickier questions," she promised.

Mr. Clark was sitting back in his chair now, his fingers steepled under his chin. Carly was clearly not excused from the hot seat. "Liked your work on the cooking contest," he said. "How would you feel about taking on more varied assignments like that one? We're thinking of picking up one of the syndicated advice columns instead of running our own, you see."

Carly could barely keep from leaping over the desk and kissing Mr. Clark. "I would enjoy that," she said moderately.

"Good, good," responded the editor as his phone buzzed. As he reached for the receiver, he mused, more to himself than to Carly, "Maybe we'll put you on the fathers' rights piece with Holbrook. Get a woman's side of it."

Carly nodded. She wasn't sure how she felt about working with Mark—God knew, he was a genius and she'd kill for the opportunity to learn from him, but he was also the man who had taken her to bed the night before and calmly turned her inside out. If she did get to share the assignment, she would just have to make damn sure she kept her mind on business.

Mr. Clark dismissed her with a kindly gesture, and she rushed out of his office, feeling better than she had all day. When she returned to her desk, she found a turkey sandwich from the corner deli waiting for her, along with a note. "Eat this that others might live. Mark."

Carly couldn't help smiling. She sat down at her desk and made short work of the sandwich, then spent the rest of the afternoon conferring with experts over the telephone. She was determined that that week's column wouldn't generate a storm of protest like the first one had.

If Mark was still in the building, he didn't come near Carly again, and she was both relieved and disappointed as she caught the elevator to the parking garage at five-thirty. She scolded herself that she mustn't fall into the age-old female trap of expecting too much just because she and Mark had been to bed together. He had probably put a check by her name in his book of conquests and moved on to the next prospect.

The thought made Carly sad, and she was feeling moody again when she got home. There, she dumped her garment bag, kicked off her shoes and exchanged the clothes she'd worn to the office for a pair of stretchy exercise pants and a leotard. What she needed, she decided, was a good workout.

After fetching a clean towel from the linen closet, she went downstairs to the building's small but well-equipped gymnasium and began going through the program she'd outlined for herself. When she was finished, she felt better.

She encountered Janet in the upstairs hallway. "You're the first woman I've ever known who looked good in sweat," her friend commented with a shake of her head.

Carly blushed, thinking of the last time she'd been worked up enough to perspire, and opened the door of her apartment. "Gee, thanks," she said with a grin. "And here I thought I didn't have anything going for me."

Janet laughed and set her briefcase and purse down on Carly's table. "Right. You were Miss United States and now you're dating a famous journalist. You're a pathetic case if I've ever seen one."

Opening her refrigerator door, Carly took out two diet colas and set them on the table. "I'm not 'dating' Mark Holbrook," she said.

Janet's lips twitched a little; she was obviously fighting back a smile. "I can't understand why you're so touchy about this, Carly—most women would shout it from the rooftops. After all, the guy is merely sensational."

Carly filled two glasses with ice and brought them to the table, sitting down with a sigh. She shrugged, averting her eyes. "He has this affectionate contempt for me, Janet—I know he sees me as a brainless little beauty queen in way over her head—"

"But," Janet pointed out moderately, "you spent the night with him."

"I don't know how to explain that," Carly said with a weary sigh.

"You don't have to explain it," Janet reasoned. "You're a grown woman, after all."

Carly bit her lower lip for a moment. Janet was right, of course, but she still felt a need to confide her feelings to someone, and she couldn't think of a better candidate than her best friend. "I never had any trouble turning guys down when they came on to me," she said quietly. "Even with Reggie—well, it was just easy to say no. But all Mark has to do is kiss me and I turn into this—this red-hot mama."

Janet let out a peal of laughter. "*Red-hot mama?* God, I didn't think anybody said that anymore!"

Carly flushed. "Janet, this is serious!" she hissed. "That man can try to get me fired, he can make remarks about my title, he can as much as tell me I'm incompetent. And then he just turns right around and takes me to bed! Doesn't that make me a woman-who-loves-too-much or something?"

Her friend was kindly amused. "Maybe it just makes you a woman-who-loves, period. Give yourself a break, Carly, and stop analyzing everything to death." She paused and glanced at her watch. "Are we still going out for salad and pizza?"

Carly nodded. "It'll have to be an early night, though. I've got a lot of work to do."

With that, Janet went to her own apartment to change clothes and Carly headed for the shower. Twenty minutes later she was dressed in gray corduroy slacks and a soft matching sweater, and the doorbell rang. Tossing her makeup bag into a drawer, she made her way through the living room and pulled open the door, expecting to see Janet standing in the hall.

Instead she found Mark, and he didn't look well.

"What's the matter?" Carly asked, stepping back to admit him.

He moved his eyes over her with weary admiration. "It's a personal problem—nothing you need to worry about."

Carly closed the door. "Then why are you here?"

He shoved one hand through his rumpled brown hair. "I'm not sure. I guess—after last night—I thought I could talk to you."

She came to stand in front of him and looked up into his eyes. "You were right—you can."

"You're on your way out." There was no note of accusation in his voice, only a quiet statement of fact.

"Janet and I are going to a pizza place, that's all. You're welcome to come along."

He grinned in a way that tugged at her heart. "Thanks, Barnett, but I don't think I'm up to snappy repartee."

She laid her hands on his upper arms. "Talk to me," she said softly.

He sighed again. "My mother called me an hour ago. Jeanine—that's my ex-wife—was in an accident on the freeway. Nathan was with her, and he's in the hospital with a broken arm."

Carly's eyes went wide with sympathy and alarm. "Then you've got to go down there."

"It isn't that simple."

"Why not? Nathan is your son—he's a little boy, and he's hurt—"

"And his mother has a restraining order against me."

Carly was quiet for a long time, absorbing the implications. "You were violent?" she asked in a whisper, and even as she uttered the words, she couldn't imagine Mark doing any of the things that usually prompted ex-wives to take legal measures to protect themselves and their children.

"No, but I was angry—damn angry. And that was all Jeanine needed. She went to a lawyer and told him I was dangerous."

Carly let her forehead rest against Mark's shoulder for a moment, breathing in concert with him, feeling his frustration and pain in a strange, fundamental way. Finally she looked up at him with tears in her eyes. "Do you want me to go with you?"

He smiled, pulled her close and kissed the top of her head. "No," he said. "I just need to know you're thinking about me, and that you'll be here when I get back."

"Mark—"

He tilted her chin up and gave her a soft, hungry kiss, and all the reactions Carly feared so much immediately set in. If he'd wanted her then and there, she would have given herself to him, and the idea frightened her.

"I'll call," he said.

Carly only nodded and followed Mark to the door, watching him as he left. Janet came in almost unobserved, dressed in designer jeans and a sweatshirt.

"Looks serious," she remarked.

"Let's go get some pizza," Carly replied.

Although Carly tried to have fun with her friend, she was essentially preoccupied. She and Janet came home early.

When she arrived at work the next morning, she stopped by Mark's office, being as subtle as possible, and peeked in. The place was spacious and cluttered, and it smelled of Mark's cologne. And it was empty.

She stepped out, closing the door and wondering how this man had made her care so deeply in such a short time. She had too much of herself invested in Mark, and she had no idea how to back away.

There were flowers waiting on her desk—pink daisies exploding from a pretty cut-glass vase. *It's too soon to talk about love,* the card read, *but I think I'm seriously in like. With you, of course. I left the key to my front door with your secretary, just in case you might want to be there when I get home. Soon, Mark.*

A rush of feeling swept over Carly. She put it down to "like" and switched on her computer.

When Emmeline came in with the customary cup of coffee, she brought the key to Mark's house. To her credit, the secretary neither asked questions nor made a comment.

Carly spent a busy day reading letters and talking with various authorities, and when her deadline arrived, she had a solid column to turn in.

She went to Mark's that first night, which was silly because she knew he wouldn't be there. She walked through the house, checking to make sure all the doors and windows were locked, then sat down at his desk.

One of the drawers was sticking out, and Carly tried to close it.

It promptly jammed, and she reached inside.

She hadn't actually meant to snoop. Still, when Carly drew her hand out of the drawer, there was a manuscript in it.

Carly realized she'd found a printout of the play he'd been writing, and she couldn't resist flipping to the opening scene. She would just read a line or two, then put it away.

Moments later, however, Carly was in another dimension. She wasn't aware of time passing, or of the dying light at the windows, or the view of the Columbia River. She read, filled with awe and a singular heartbreak, to the very last page.

Tears brimmed in her eyes as she put the play back in its drawer, and just then the phone rang. Feeling like a prowler, but nonetheless a responsible one, Carly groped for the receiver and sniffled, "Hello?"

"Hi." The voice was Mark's.

Carly gave a guilty start and dashed away her tears with the back of one hand, trying to cover her discomfort with a joke. "Your burglar alarm doesn't work," she said.

He chuckled. "I didn't turn it on. I'm glad you're there, Carly—it's almost as good as having you here would be."

"How's Nathan? Did you get to see him?"

"One question at a time, Scoop. Nathan's going to be fine—I think I'm in worse shape than he is."

"And Jeanine?"

Mark hesitated for a long moment. "She's as difficult as ever."

"But she wasn't hurt in the accident?"

"No."

"What about the restraining order? Was there any trouble?"

"I called my parents' attorney when I got here and had it lifted. I'll tell you all about it when I get home tomorrow night."

Carly felt a wifely warmth at the idea. "Maybe I'll stop by after work, then," she said.

Mark's voice was a slow, sensual caress. "Bring your toothbrush."

She squirmed slightly and let the remark pass. "Thanks for the flowers—they're lovely."

They talked for a few minutes longer, then said reluctant good-nights.

During the drive back to her apartment, Carly thought about Mark's play. His talent was truly formidable, and his words had moved her on a very deep level. She should have told him that she'd read his work, she knew, but the truth was she hadn't dared. The play was about a man and a woman and a child, and in it the dissolution of the family had been portrayed with painful clarity.

It didn't take a genius to figure out that Mark had written about his own divorce, or that he felt a tragic sense of loss where his young son was concerned.

The subject of Mark's previous marriage seemed to be sacred ground; Carly didn't know how to broach it. She felt almost as though she'd read his diary, tapped his phone or opened his mail. And yet there was a certain exaltation in her, too, because the play had such a poignant beauty.

Arriving at her own building, Carly carried in her purse, briefcase and mail. There was a wedding invitation from Reggie and the nurse from Topeka, and she rolled her eyes as she tossed it onto the desk with the other things.

After changing her clothes, Carly again went to the small gym to work out. When she returned, she showered, made herself a light supper and started reading the briefcase full of misery she'd brought home from the office.

Although she tried, Carly was unable to keep her mind on the letters from readers of her column. Her thoughts kept straying to Mark, and his play. She wanted so much to tell him she'd read it, and that it was wonderful.

But she was afraid.

The next day was hectic, as usual, and Carly didn't have time to think about anything but her work. At six-thirty she got into her car, where a small suitcase and her beauty case were waiting, and drove to Mark's place, stopping off at a supermarket on the way.

When she reached his isolated house, there was no sign of his car, though the compact pickup was parked in its usual place.

She unlocked the door and went inside. "Mark?" she called out in a hopeful tone of voice, but there was no answer.

Carly carried her luggage into Mark's room, changed into jeans and a T-shirt, then went back to the living room. With considerable effort, she managed to start a blaze in the fireplace, and she found a Mozart tape and put it on the stereo.

She was in the kitchen, chopping vegetables for a salad, when she saw his car swing into the driveway. Her heart leaped with an excitement it wasn't entitled to, and she hurried out to meet him.

He needed a shave, and he looked haggard, but his grin transformed his face. "Hi, Scoop," he said hoarsely when she slipped her arms around his waist.

Carly reached up to touch his cheek. "Aren't you going to kiss me?"

He laughed and gathered her against him, and when his mouth touched Carly's, it was as though someone had draped a wet towel over an electric fence. The charge was lethal.

She was breathless when he finally released her. "I hope you didn't eat on the plane," she managed to say, "because I want to cook for you tonight."

Mark reached into the car for his suitcase and assumed a look of comical surprise. "You cook, as well as twirl the baton and tell total strangers to get divorced?" he teased. "My God, Barnett—is there no end to your talents?"

She gave him a saucy look over one shoulder as she led the way toward the gaping front door. "I've got talents galore."

He laughed and followed her into the house.

While Carly broiled the steaks she'd bought, and baked the potatoes, Mark showered and changed clothes. When he joined her on the little patio off the kitchen, he was wearing jeans and a football jersey, and his rich brown hair was still damp.

"I could get used to this," he said, standing behind Carly and slipping his arms around her waist. His lips were warm and tantalizing against her neck.

Carly pretended to bristle, though the fact was that she wouldn't have protested if Mark had hauled her off to bed right then. "You're a chauvinist, Mr. Holbrook."

"I know," he said, lifting her hair to kiss her lightly on the nape.

She was trembling when she turned in his arms and gazed into his eyes. She had to tell him she'd read his play now, while things were so good between them. "Mark, I—"

He silenced her by laying an index finger to her lips. "Later," he told her. "Whatever it is, please save it until after the food, and the loving."

During the meal Carly and Mark didn't talk about Nathan, or Mark's trip. Instead they discussed some of the funnier letters Carly had received and the answers she'd been tempted to give.

They laughed, and the sound of it healed injured places deep inside Carly. Once, tears came to her eyes because it felt so good just to be sitting across the picnic table from Mark, watching the changes in his face as he talked or listened.

He was rinsing their dishes and putting them into the machine when Carly told him the advice column might be discontinued. She watched closely for his reaction, then felt relief when he grinned and said, "They'll probably find a place for you."

Carly drew a deep breath and leaned against the breakfast bar. "Actually," she said, "they already have, sort of."

Mark looked at her curiously. "Don't keep me in suspense, Scoop—are they sending you on assignment to the White House or what?"

She ran the tip of her tongue over her lips. "I'm probably going to be working with you," she answered, "on a piece about fathers' rights. Mr. Clark wanted a woman's view on the subject."

He sighed, slammed the dishwasher door closed and shoved one hand through his hair. "Great."

Carly went to him and laid her hand gently on his arm. "Mark, I'm not Jeanine," she said in a quiet voice. "I don't have any axes to grind."

He drew her close and buried his face in her hair. "I missed you so much," he said hoarsely.

5

Mark knelt in front of the fireplace, adding wood to the blaze, while Carly sat on the suede couch, her legs curled beneath her. The white wine in her glass sparkled and winked like a liquid jewel.

"Things are happening pretty fast between us," she said.

He looked back at her over one shoulder. "Is that a problem?"

Carly thought, taking a leisurely sip of her wine. "Yeah, when you consider we don't even know what it is."

Mark joined her on the couch, taking her wineglass from her hand and setting it beside his on the coffee table. "Don't look now, Barnett, but I think it's passion," he said, easing Carly down onto the cushions and then poising himself over her.

He was so incredibly brazen, but Carly couldn't find it in her heart to protest. She wanted to feel his weight pressing down on her, wanted to lose herself in the multicolored light show his lovemaking would set off in her head.

Mark drank the wine from her lips, then shaped her mouth with his and delved into her with his tongue. Carly felt as though he'd already taken her, and an electrical jolt racked her body. With a whimper, she flung her arms around his neck and responded without reservation.

Mark was gasping when he broke the kiss and slid downward over her body. Carly raised her T-shirt and opened her bra of her own accord, and his groan of pleasure at the sight of her naked breasts vibrated under her flesh.

She cried out in acquiescence when he caught one of her nipples in his mouth and grazed it lightly with his teeth, and dug her fingers into his muscular back.

Before, Mark had taken his sweet time loving her, but that night there was a primitive urgency between them that would brook no delays. While he drank from her breast, Mark was unsnapping her jeans and pushing them down.

She kicked off her shoes, and Mark relieved her of the jeans. She lay before him in just her underpants, with her bra unhooked and her T-shirt bunched under her armpits, and for all the indignity of that she felt beautiful because his brown eyes moved over her with reverence.

"Take me," she whispered, letting the backs of her hands rest against the soft suede of the couch on either side of her head.

He bent his head and nipped at her lightly through the silky fabric of her panties until she was moaning softly and beginning to writhe.

Then his clothes were gone as quickly as Carly's. He knelt between her legs, hooking his thumbs under the waistband of her panties, drawing them downward.

"Don't think you're going to get off this easy, Scoop," he teased, finding her entrance and placing himself there. His eyes glittered with desire as he gazed down into her face. "I plan to keep you busy for a long time."

Carly groaned as he gave her an inch then she clawed frantically at his bare back. "Please, Mark—don't make me wait—"

His response was a long, fierce stroke that took him to her very depths. He cupped his hands beneath her bottom, lifting her into position for another thrust.

"Faster," Carly fretted.

He chuckled. "Does this mean you missed me?"

"Damn you, Mark Holbrook!"

After that, he loved her in earnest, with fire and fever, and when the hot storm broke within her, she sobbed his name.

He covered her face with light, frantic kisses as he climaxed, his mouth on her eyelids, her cheeks, the underside of her chin. In those treacherous moments, Carly felt cherished as well as thoroughly mastered.

When it was over, he fell to her, taking solace in her softness in the age-old way of men. His breath came hard and his words, spoken against her cheek, were labored. "If this gets . . . any better . . . I'm going to need . . . respiratory therapy."

Carly laughed softly and laid her hands to either side of his face. "Look at me, Mark. I've got to tell you something before I lose my courage."

He raised his head, his brown eyes mischievous. "You used to be a man," he guessed.

Carly's delight erupted in another burst of amusement. "Wrong."

"You have a prison record."

She couldn't let the game go on any longer. "I read your play, Mark," she blurted out. "I found it and I read it."

He studied her somberly for a long time, then thrust himself upward and reached for his clothes.

"Mark?"

"I heard you, Carly."

"I don't blame you for being angry—I shouldn't have snooped. But it was fabulous—really fabulous."

He got back into his jeans and stormed across the room to his desk.

Carly dressed awkwardly while he wrenched open the drawer, found the screenplay and flung it toward her, its fanfold pages spreading out over the floor. "Mark—"

"You like it?" he rasped. "It's yours. Take it. Line bird cages with it!"

"What is the matter with you?" Carly demanded, snapping her jeans. When he didn't answer, but just stood gazing out through the dark windows, she knelt and gently gathered the play up from the floor. She handled it like the broken pieces of something she'd cherished. "Do you know what I'd give to be able to write like this?"

He turned around then, and to Carly's relief he was much calmer. "You'd have had to feel the pain," he said. "Believe me, the price is too high."

She held the manuscript to her breast like a child as she stood. "I *did* feel the pain, Mark—that's what makes it such a wonderful piece of work—"

"Look," Mark interrupted sharply, "I don't give a damn that you read it, all right? But it represents another part of my life and I can't talk about it—I don't want to be reminded."

"I can keep it?" Carly ventured cautiously. "I can take it home?"

"Do whatever you want."

Carly was filled with sadness as she carried the play across the room and tucked it into her briefcase. She should have known Mark would be angry; she'd been trespassing in the deepest reaches of his soul.

"Carly?"

She felt his hands, strong and gentle, on her shoulders. "I'm sorry, Mark," she whispered.

He turned her to face him. "No," he said huskily. "I'm the one who was wrong. I apologize."

She managed a broken smile. "We both knew this wasn't going to work, didn't we?" she asked.

He gave her a slight shake. "Of course it's going to work," he argued. "It has to."

She prayed she wouldn't cry. "Why?"

"Because I need you, and I hope to God you need me, that's why. Because I think maybe I love you."

"You 'think maybe'?" Carly asked, hugging herself. She felt shaky and confused. "What the hell kind of statement is that?"

Mark caught her by the belt loops at the front of her jeans and hauled her toward him. "I'm doing the best I can here, Carly, so how about helping me out a little?" he said, his face very close to hers. "I don't *know* if this feeling is love—I don't even know if there's any such thing as romantic love—

but damn it, I feel *something* for the first time in ten years and I don't want it to stop!''

Carly drew a deep, shaky breath. "You're probably just horny," she said in a tone of resignation.

Mark laughed like a comical maniac, hoisted her up over one shoulder and gave her a sound swat on the bottom. "You may be right," he agreed.

"Put me down!" Carly gasped. "I'm about to throw up."

"I love these romantic moments," Mark answered, carrying her toward his bedroom in exactly the same position. "I feel like Errol Flynn."

"You're an idiot!"

He hauled her up the steps to his bed and flung her down on the mattress. "Will you lighten up, Scoop? Something poignant is happening here."

"Like what?"

Mark stretched out beside her. "Damned if I know, but like I said—I sure don't want it to end."

Carly didn't know whether she was happy or sad, whether she wanted to laugh or cry, but tears filled her eyes and she said, "Hold me."

The next morning, she was careful to go to work in her own car, hoping no one at the newspaper would guess what was going on between her and Mark. But that night she went back to his house, and he cooked spaghetti.

They laughed and talked and made love, but they didn't discuss Mark's play. Or the assignment they might be sharing.

Friday was hectic. The decision to end the advice column had been made, and Carly felt responsible for its demise to some degree. After all, there had been the "Frazzled in Farleyville" incident.

She still had her office, however, and Mr. Clark announced in a special staff meeting that she and Mark would be working together for the time being. Carly could not have been happier, but there was something disturbing about the remote look she saw in Mark's eyes when he looked at her.

"We'll start working on the story tonight," he announced peremptorily, when everyone else had left the conference room.

Carly swallowed. "I can't."

He raised his eyebrows. "You can't?" he echoed, with a maddeningly indulgent note in his voice. "Why not, pray tell?"

Carly dragged in a deep breath and let it out with a whoosh. "I've got a dinner date. Jim Benson, remember? Channel 37?"

Mark walked over to the door and calmly pushed it shut. "Break it," he said.

Hot pink indignation throbbed in Carly's cheeks. "I beg your pardon."

He was glaring at her. "You heard me, Carly."

Carly had no feelings for Jim Benson one way or the other. She just wanted to establish contacts, to "network" the way other people in the media did. She struggled to stay calm. "Look, it's no big deal. Besides, when I made this date, there was nothing going on between you and me."

"And now there is," Mark pointed out evenly.

Carly laid her hand on his arm. "It's only dinner," she said, and then she left the conference room.

Mark didn't follow.

Back at her apartment, as she showered and dressed, Carly decided it would probably be a good thing if she saw other men. After all, whatever it was that had flared up between her and Mark had come on fast, and she'd had little or no chance to distance herself from the situation.

The other side of that coin, of course, was that Mark would have just as much right to date other women. And the prospect didn't appeal to Carly at all.

Jim Benson arrived promptly at seven. He was tall and handsome, with dark hair and streaks of premature gray at his temples, and bright blue eyes. He took in Carly's soft yellow dress with obvious appreciation.

As she and Jim were leaving the apartment, they encountered Janet, who stood there in the hallway, clutching a grocery bag and staring at them with her mouth open.

Carly knew there would be a message on her answering machine when she got home. "My best friend, Janet McClain," she explained as she and Jim descended in the elevator.

Jim laughed. "When people gape like that, I get this overwhelming compulsion to see if my fly's open."

Jim's car, a sleek sports model, was waiting in the parking lot, and he chivalrously opened the door for her. He turned out to be a very nice guy, the kind of man Carly might have gotten serious about if she hadn't met Mark first.

When they'd reached the restaurant and were settled at their table, Jim said very companionably, "You must know Mark Holbrook, if you work at the *Times*."

Carly nodded thoughtfully. "Sometimes I wonder how well," she murmured.

"He and I have been good friends for a long time," Jim went on. "I hope you won't mind that I invited him and his date to join us for drinks later."

Carly had been sipping ice water, and she nearly choked at this announcement. "Tell me the truth," she said when she'd composed herself. "You didn't invite Mark—he invited himself."

Jim grinned. "Well . . ."

Carly had picked up her table napkin during her choking spell; now she tossed it down angrily. "Why that sneaky—"

"Am I missing something here?" the newscaster asked politely.

Carly sighed. Jim was too nice; she wasn't going to play games with him. "The truth is, Mark and I have been seeing each other, and something's going on. I don't know whether it's love or not, but it's pretty heavy, and he was upset when I told him I was keeping my date with you."

A grin spread across Jim's face. "So he just wants to unsettle you?"

"I'm afraid so," Carly said with a nod and another sigh. "I'm sorry, Jim."

He shrugged. "No reason we can't be friends." He picked up his menu and opened it. "The shrimp scampi is good here."

Carly had no appetite at all now that she knew Mark was going to show up at any minute, but she ordered the shrimp and did her best to eat.

She and Jim were in the lounge, later, when he said, "Don't look now, but your partner just walked in. Let's dance and give him a thing or two to think about."

The idea sounded good to Carly. She smiled warmly and allowed Jim to lead her onto the small dance floor. Even though it nearly killed her, she didn't look to see who Mark was with.

"Is he watching?" she asked.

Jim chuckled and drew her closer. "Oh, yes. If that expression in his eyes were a laser beam, he'd be doing surgery on me. The kind you don't recover from."

Carly laughed. "And the woman?"

"Weatherperson from Channel 18. Very cute."

Before Carly could maneuver into a position where she could get a look at Mark's date, he walked right onto the dance floor. Carly was pulled from Jim's arms into Mark's long before he took the trouble to grind out, "May I cut in?"

"No," Carly answered, but when she tried to pull away, he restrained her. "This is ridiculous."

He arched one eyebrow. "All right, I admit it— I'm jealous as hell."

Carly smiled acidly, her eyes widening in mock surprise. "No!"

He gave her a surreptitious pinch on the bottom, and she gasped and stiffened in response. "You've made your point, Barnett—I don't have any rights where you're concerned. But you're going to have to give up dating other guys, unless you want me tagging along."

"Why should I?" Carly asked. "Give up dating other guys, I mean."

"Because I l-like you."

"Well, I *l-like* you, too. Maybe I even love you. In spite of the fact that you're acting like a badly trained baboon tonight." The music stopped. "How about introducing me to your date, Mark?"

He cleared his throat, took her hand and started toward the table where Jim and the weatherperson were sitting, already deep in conversation. "I told you he was a lech," Mark whispered.

"And he told me you were his friend," Carly scolded.

"I was, until he made a move on you," Mark responded, still talking under his breath.

Jim stood when he saw Carly, and an unreadable look passed between the two men. Mark pulled out Carly's chair for her and, when she was seated, sat down beside the weatherperson.

"This is Margery Woods," he said. "Margery, Carly Barnett."

The young woman's brown eyes were round with admiration. "Miss United States, nineteen-eighty—"

"Let's not talk about me," Carly broke in.

"But I saw your pageant—I have it on tape. I tape all the pageants."

Carly looked to both Mark and Jim for rescue, but neither of them offered it. In fact, they both looked amused, as though they'd set up some tacit conspiracy. "That's—that's nice," she said. "Have you been dating Mark long, Margery?"

That question wiped the complacent look from Mark's face.

"On and off for about six months," Margery responded with a philosophical sigh. Then she gave her date an affectionately suspicious glance. "But I've heard rumors that he's running around with some bimbo at the newspaper office."

Carly managed to swallow the sip of white wine she'd taken without choking on it, but just barely. She gave Mark a look that said, *just you wait, fella,* then changed the subject.

By the time Jim drove her home, she was exhausted. "I'm sorry," she said again at her door. "Tonight was probably a real drag for you."

He smiled and kissed her lightly on the forehead. "Actually it was the most fun I've had in weeks. If it helps any, I can tell you that Mark's in love with you."

The words gave Carly a soft, melting feeling inside. "It helps," she said.

"That's what I was afraid of," Jim answered with a grin and a shrug. He kissed Carly again and walked away.

As soon as Carly was inside her apartment with the lights flipped on and the door locked behind her, she saw the red flicker on her answering machine. Kicking off her high-heeled shoes and pushing one hand through her hair, she padded across the room and pushed the button.

"Who was that hunk?" Janet's voice demanded without so much as a hello. "I mean, I know who he is because I've seen him on television. What I meant was, what are you doing going out with him when you've got this hot thing going with Mark Holbrook? You'd better call me *tonight*, Carly Barnett, or our friendship is over!"

Carly grinned as the machine clicked and went on to the next message.

"Carly, honey, this is your dad. I was just calling to see how you're doing. Give me a ring tomorrow sometime, if you have a chance—I'll be at the filling station."

Her throat thick, because she would have liked very much to talk with her father and maybe get some perspective on the situation with Mark, Carly sank into the desk chair to hear any further messages.

"Okay, I acted like a caveman," Mark's voice confessed. "It's pretty strange, Scoop—I'm sorry, and yet I know I'd do the same thing all over again. I'll pick you up in the morning for breakfast and we'll get started on the new project. Bye."

After that, the machine rewound and Carly shut it off. She wondered what her dad would think of

Mark Holbrook and his high-handed but virtually irresistible methods. Her teeth sinking into her lower lip, Carly glanced at the clock on her desk and wished it wasn't so late in Kansas.

The sudden jangling of the telephone startled her so much that she nearly fell off her chair. Knowing the caller was probably either Mark or Janet, she answered with a somewhat snappish "Hello."

"Hi, baby," her father's voice said.

"Dad!" Carly looked at the clock again. "Is everything okay? Are you sick?"

He chuckled. "Do I have to be sick to call my little girl?"

Carly let out a long sigh. "I'm so glad you did," she said. "I really need to talk to you."

"I'm listening."

Carly's eyes stung with tears of love and home-sickness. Her dad had always been willing to listen, and she was grateful. "I think I'm falling in love, Dad. His name is Mark Holbrook, and he's utterly obnoxious, but I can't stay away from him."

Her father laughed affectionately. "Did you think it would be bad news to me, your falling in love? I'm happy for you, honey."

"Didn't you hear me, Dad? I said he was obnoxious! And he is. He's got this Pulitzer prize, and he's always making comments about my title—"

"There are worse problems."

"I think he's going to ask me to move in with him," Carly burst out.

Don Barnett was quiet for several moments. "If he does, what are you going to say?"

Carly swallowed hard. "Yes. I think."

If her father had made any private judgments, he didn't voice them. "You're a big girl now, Carly. You have to make decisions like that for yourself."

Carly sighed. "Maybe I should hold out for white lace and promises," she mused.

Her dad chuckled at that. "Even when you've got those things, there aren't any guarantees. The name of the game is risk."

It seemed like a good time to change the subject. "Speaking of risk, Dad," Carly began with a smile in her voice, "are you still eating your meals over at Mad Bill's Café?"

He laughed. "Bill's going to be real hurt when I tell him you said that."

Five minutes later, an impatient knock at Carly's door terminated the conversation. She said goodbye to her father, went to the peephole and looked out.

Her arms folded, Janet was standing in the hallway, wearing her corduroy bathrobe.

Carly opened the door, and her friend swept into the room.

"You didn't call," Janet accused.

"I was talking with my dad," Carly answered, grinning as she went into the kitchen to put on the teakettle. A nice cup of chamomile would help her sleep.

Janet followed her into the kitchenette. "Well? What's going on? Is it over between you and Mark?"

Carly chuckled and shook her head. "No, but it sure is complicated. Jim is just an acquaintance, Janet—I want to make contacts."

There was a pause while Janet inspected her freshly polished fingernails and Carly got mugs down from the cupboard, along with a box of herbal tea bags. "Maybe you could fix me up with him," she finally said. "Jim, I mean."

Carly smiled. "Sure," she said gently. "I'll see what I can do."

"You're a true friend," Janet beamed. But then she glanced at her watch and frowned. "I'd better not stay for tea—I'm putting in some overtime tomorrow. Let me know when things are set."

"I will," Carly promised, following Janet to the door and closing and locking it behind her.

It was very late and Carly had to be up early the next morning herself, but even after drinking the chamomile tea, she couldn't go to sleep. She got

Mark's play out, carried it to bed and began to read.

Again she was awed by the scope of the man's talent—and a little jealous, too. No matter how hard she worked, it would be years before she was even in the same ballpark. In fact, in her heart Carly knew she would never be the caliber of journalist Mark was, and she wondered if she would be able to live with that fact and accept it.

Long after she had set the play aside and turned out the light, Carly lay in the darkness, thinking about it, envisioning it produced on a stage or movie screen. It would be remarkable in either medium.

A wild idea she barely dared to entertain came to her. The temptation to send the work to an agent was almost overpowering. After all, Mark had said the play was hers, that she could do what she wanted to with it.

Carly sighed. He'd been upset at the time.

Finally, after much tossing and turning, she was able to go to sleep.

It seemed to Carly that no more than five minutes could have passed when her eyes were suddenly flooded with spring sunlight from the window facing her bed. At the same time, Mark—it had to be Mark—was leaning on the doorbell.

Grabbing for her robe, Carly shrugged into it and went grumpily to the door. Sure enough, the peephole revealed Mark standing in the hallway.

Carly let him in, prepared for a lecture.

"You're not ready," he pointed. "What kind of reporter are you, Barnett? There's a whole world out there living, dying, loving and fighting. And here you are—" his eyes ran mischievously over her pink bathrobe "—standing around looking like a giant piece of cotton candy."

Carly retreated a step and cinched her belt tighter. She knew the perils of standing too close to Mark Holbrook in a bathrobe. "I'll be ready in ten minutes," she said.

"Make it five," Mark retorted, glancing pointedly at his watch. "We have a plane to catch."

Carly stared at him. "A plane?"

Mark nodded, his hands tucked into his hip pockets. "If we're going to write about fathers' rights, Scoop, you're going to have to do a little research on the subject. We'll start by introducing you to Nathan."

"But I can't just leave—"

"Why do you think Clark gave me this story?" Mark interrupted. "He knows I've got my guts invested in it. And you're my assistant. Therefore, where I go, you go. Now hurry up."

Carly hurried into the bathroom, showered, and hastily styled her hair and put on light makeup. After that, she pulled a suitcase out from under the bed.

"How long are we going to be gone?" she called out.

Mark appeared in her doorway. He was sipping a cup of coffee, and he looked impossibly attractive in his jeans and Irish cable-knit sweater. "Long enough for you to see that women aren't the only ones who sometimes have their rights trampled on," he responded.

Carly wasn't about to comment on that one—not before breakfast. She packed as sensibly as she could, tucking the play into her suitcase when Mark wasn't looking, and left a message on Janet's machine saying she'd be away on business for a while. Finally she and Mark set out for the airport in his car.

After they'd bought their tickets and checked in their baggage, they went to a busy restaurant for breakfast. Carly left the table for a few minutes, and when she returned, there was a long velvet box beside her orange juice.

Her hand trembled a little as she reached for it and lifted the lid to find a bracelet of square gold links. She was unable to speak when she lifted her eyes to Mark's face.

He took the bracelet from the box and deftly clasped it around her wrist. "I can't pretend this trip is strictly business, Carly," he said, his eyes warm and serious. "I guess what it all boils down to is, I'm asking you to move in with me."

6

"I need some time to think," Carly said softly, gazing down at the bracelet in stricken wonder. The words sounded odd even to her, especially in light of what she'd told her father the night before, about saying yes if Mark asked her to live with him. Being confronted with the reality was something quite different, though, and whatever it was that she and Mark had together was still fragile. She didn't want to ruin it.

She was trying to unfasten the bracelet when Mark's fingers stopped her.

"It's all right, Carly," he said quietly. "No matter what you decide, I want you to keep the bracelet."

They finished their breakfast in a silence that was at once awkward and cordial, then went to board their plane.

Once they were settled in their seats and their aircraft had taken off, Mark was all business. He pulled a notebook and a couple of pens from his briefcase and started outlining his basic ideas about the piece on fathers' rights. He listened to Carly's input thoughtfully and even condescended to use some of it.

By the time they landed in San Francisco, they had the basic structure of the article sketched in.

In the cab that brought them into the city, they argued. Mark naturally felt that fathers got a bad deal, as a general rule, when it came to questions like custody and visitation rights. Carly responded that he was prejudiced, that many fathers didn't care enough about their children to pay support, let alone visit or seek custody.

The taxi came to a stop in front of an elegant house overlooking the Bay, and Carly was surprised. She hadn't paid attention when Mark gave directions to the cabdriver.

"We're not staying in a hotel?"

Mark grinned as he held the car door open for her. "My parents would regard it as an insult," he answered.

Soon they were standing on the sidewalk with their luggage, the cab speeding away down the hill. And Carly was nervous.

"This isn't fair, Mark. You didn't warn me that I was going to be meeting your family."

"You didn't ask," he said as a plump woman in a maid's uniform opened the front door and came out onto the porch.

"They're here!" she called back over one shoulder.

Mark was holding Carly's suitcase, but she grabbed it. "How are you going to present me?" she whispered out of the side of her mouth. "As the woman you want to live with?"

"I detect hostility," Mark whispered back just as a tall, striking lady with white hair came out of the house, beaming with delight.

Carly knew immediately that this was Mark's mother, and she smiled nervously as Mrs. Holbrook kissed her son's cheek. "It's so good to see you again, darling."

"It's only been a few days, Mom," Mark pointed out, but the look in his eyes was affectionate. "This is Carly," he added, slipping his free arm around her waist.

Carly smiled and offered her hand. "Hello."

Mrs. Holbrook's grasp was firm and friendly. "Welcome, Carly. I'm very pleased to meet you." She turned resigned eyes to Mark. "There is a problem, though."

"What?" Mark asked, starting toward the door.

Mrs. Holbrook stopped him with two words. "Jeanine's here."

Carly felt a wild urge to turn and chase the taxi down the street.

Mark paused on the step, frowning down into his mother's concerned face. "What the—"

Before he could finish, a tall beauty with auburn hair and Irish green eyes appeared in the doorway. Her complexion was flawless, and her gaze moved over Mark in a proprietary way, then strayed to Carly.

"So," she said, her voice icy. "This is Mark's beauty queen."

Although the words had not been particularly inflammatory, Carly felt as though she'd been slapped. She lifted her chin and met Jeanine's gaze straight on, though she didn't speak.

Mrs. Holbrook linked her arm through Carly's and politely propelled her toward the door, forcing Jeanine to shrink back into the entryway. "Don't be rude, dear," she said evenly. "Carly is my guest."

The maid led the way up the stairs, depositing Carly in a lovely room decorated in muted mauve and ivory. There was an inner door that probably led to Mark's quarters.

Sure enough, he came through it five seconds after Carly had popped open her suitcase.

"I should have warned you," he said, giving her a light kiss on the mouth. "Here be dragons, milady."

"Thanks a lot," Carly said furiously. She was still smarting because Jeanine had called her a "beauty queen," and because she had a pretty good idea where the description had come from.

Mark's eyes were dancing as he shrugged and spread his hands. "Don't feel bad, Scoop—I didn't like her, either. That's why we were divorced."

"How did she know we were coming?" Carly demanded in a furious whisper.

Mark sighed and sat down on the edge of Carly's four-poster bed. "Mom probably told her."

"It must be nice to be let in on little things like that!" Carly spat, pacing. She had half a mind to call a cab and head straight for the airport. The trouble was, half a mind wasn't enough for the task.

Mark reached out and pulled her easily onto his lap. She struggled, he restrained her, and she gave up with an angry huff.

He unbuttoned her blouse far enough to kiss the cleft between her breasts, resting his hand lightly on her thigh.

Carly felt as though someone had doused her in kerosene, then touched a match to her. "Mark, not here. Not now."

"Umm-hmm," he agreed, pushing down her bra on one side and nonchalantly taking her nipple into his mouth.

She stiffened on his lap, unwilling to free herself from his spell even though she knew it was desperately important to do so. "Mark," she moaned in feeble protest.

He raised her linen skirt, and dipped his hand inside her tap pants and the top of her panty hose. His lips never left her breast. "Umm," he said.

Carly swallowed a strangled cry of delighted protest as he found her secret and began to toy with it. "You—are—an absolute—*bastard,*" she panted.

He chuckled and nuzzled her other breast, nipping at it through the thin, lacy fabric of her bra. "No question about it," he admitted. And he slid his fingers inside Carly and plied her with his thumb.

She clutched his shoulders, and a soft sob of rebellious submission escaped her as he worked his singular magic. She felt a fine mist of perspiration on her upper lip and between her breasts as he made her body respond to him. She let her head fall back in surrender. "So—arrogant—"

He slipped his tongue beneath the top of her bra to find her nipple. "You love it," he said when he paused to bare her for his leisurely enjoyment.

That was the worst part of it, Carly thought, writhing helplessly under Mark's attentions. She *did* love it.

Her climax was a noisy one, despite her efforts to swallow her cries of release, and Mark muffled it by covering her mouth with his own. When she sagged against him in a sated stupor, he withdrew his hand and calmly fastened her bra, buttoned her blouse and straightened her skirt.

When he set her on her feet, she swayed, and he steadied her by grasping her hips in his hands.

He stood, kissed her gently on the mouth, then disappeared into his room.

Mark hadn't been gone five minutes when a light knock sounded at the outer door. Carly had been sitting on the window seat, staring out at the Bay and wondering whether what she felt for Mark was love or obsession, and she was grateful for a distraction.

"Come in," she said quietly.

Mrs. Holbrook stepped into the room. "Lunch is nearly ready," she said with a smile. "I do hope you're hungry, my dear. Eleanor makes a very nice crab salad sandwich."

Carly smiled lamely and hoped her clothes weren't rumpled from those wild minutes on Mark's lap. "That sounds marvelous," she answered. She didn't have the courage to ask if Jeanine was still present and, fortunately, she didn't have to.

"Jeanine is gone, for the time being at least," Mrs. Holbrook volunteered. "I should have known better than to tell her I was expecting you and Mark."

Carly lowered her eyes for a moment. The phrase "beauty queen" was still lodged in her mind like a nettle, and she wondered why Mark hadn't spoken of her as a journalist, or even an assistant. It hurt to be defined with a long-defunct pageant title when she'd worked so hard to learn to write. "It's all right, Mrs. Holbrook," she said.

"Please," the woman said gently, holding out a hand to Carly. "Call me Helen. And what do you say we give Mark the slip and have our sandwiches in the garden? He's on the telephone with his father."

Carly smiled and nodded, and she and Helen went downstairs together.

The garden turned out to be a terrace lined with budding rosebushes and blooming pink azaleas. There was a glass-topped table with a pink-and-white umbrella and a splendid view of the Golden Gate. A salty breeze blew in from the water, rippling Carly's hair, and she had a strange sensation of returning home after a long, difficult journey.

"Did you know Mark wrote a play about his marriage and divorce?" she asked when the maid had brought their sandwiches, along with a bone-china tea service, and left again.

"I'm not surprised," Helen said, and there was a sad expression on her still-beautiful face. "He deals with most things by writing about them."

Carly had known Helen Holbrook for less than an hour, and yet she felt safe with her. "It's absolutely brilliant," she went on. Just recalling the powerful emotions the play had stirred in her almost brought tears to her eyes. "And he's not going to do anything with it."

Helen sighed. "Sometimes," she reflected, "I delude myself that I understand my son. Mostly, though, I accept the fact that he's a law unto himself."

Carly nodded. "He gave me the play," she said. "He told me I could do anything I wanted to with it—that it was mine."

Helen's gaze met Carly's, and in that instant the two women came to an understanding. "Then I guess you'd be within your rights if you took certain obvious steps," Helen said.

Before Carly could respond, Mark appeared in the gaping French doors that led from an old-fashioned, elegantly furnished parlor. He was carrying a sandwich and a tall glass of ice tea. He winked at

Carly, in a tacit reminder of the episode upstairs, bringing a blush to her cheeks.

"Jeanine's bringing Nathan over in an hour," he said.

Carly felt like an intruder, but didn't move from her chair. And she knew then that they hadn't flown to San Francisco to work on the article, but to come to terms with Mark's past.

Helen looked extremely uncomfortable. "Jeanine's been drinking more and more lately," she finally confided.

Carly was about to make an excuse and retreat to her room when Mark reached out and closed his hand over hers, indicating that he wanted her to stay. She felt a charge go through her that probably registered on the Richter scale.

"And she was drunk when she had the accident," Mark ventured.

His mother pressed her lips together in a thin line for a long moment, then said, "I think so, but she denies it, of course."

Mark slammed his fist down on the glass table-top and bounded out of his chair to stand facing the Bay, his hands gripping the stone wall that bordered the garden. "One of these days she's going to kill him."

Carly longed to help, to change things somehow, but of course there was nothing she could do.

Mark finally came back to the table, but he was too restless to sit. He put one hand on Carly's shoulder and squeezed, and she pressed her fingers over his.

Helen's lovely blue eyes moved from Carly's face to her son's. With a perceptive smile, she rose from her chair. "I think I'll make myself scarce for a little while," she announced, and then she vanished.

Carly stood and slipped her arms around Mark's waist. "I like your mother," she said.

He kissed her briefly. "So do I, but I don't think she's the topic you really want to discuss."

Carly shook her head, resting her hands on the lapels of his lightweight tweed jacket. "You're right. I want to know how you met Jeanine, and what made you fall in love with her."

"I didn't 'meet' Jeanine—I've known her all my life," Mark answered, and there was a hoarse note of resignation in his voice. "We were expected to get married, and we didn't want to disappoint anybody, so we did."

"You must have loved her once."

Mark shook his head. "I didn't know what love was," he answered huskily. "Not until Nathan came along. As soon as Jeanine realized how much I cared about our son, she began using him against me."

I know, Carly wanted to say. *I read your play.*
But she only stood there, close to Mark, her head
on his shoulder, her eyes fixed on the capricious
Bay.

"I want him back, Carly," he went on. "Not just
for weekends, or holidays or summer vacations.
For keeps."

She wasn't surprised. "From what you've said,"
she answered softly, "the chances of that aren't too
good."

"I can fight her. I can sue for custody."

Carly turned so that she could look up into
Mark's face. She saw determination there, and
fury, and she had a glimmer of what he'd meant
when he'd spoken so bitterly of fathers' rights. Her
heart went out to him. "You might lose," she said.

"Life is full of risks," he answered.

Carly and Mark were in the parlor when Jeanine
returned, bringing Nathan with her.

He was a handsome, serious boy, so like his father that Carly's heart lurched slightly when she
saw him. He was wearing jeans and a red-and-blue
striped T-shirt, and there was a cast on his left arm,
covered with writing.

He beamed, showing a gap where his two front
teeth had been. "Hi, Dad," he said a little shyly.

Carly noticed the tears in Jeanine's eyes as she
stood behind her son, and felt a moment's pity for

the woman. Perhaps Mark had been telling the truth when he said he'd never loved Jeanine, but Carly knew for certain that Jeanine had once loved him. Maybe she still did.

"Come here," Mark said huskily, and the child rushed into his arms.

"Have him back by nine o'clock," Jeanine said crisply, her chin high. "And don't give him sugar. It makes him hyper."

Mark ruffled his son's rich brown hair and nodded at Jeanine, and that was the extent of his civility. Carly was relieved when the other woman left the room.

"I want you to meet somebody," Mark told the boy, putting an arm around Nathan's shoulder and gently turning him toward Carly. "This is my— friend, Carly Barnett. Carly, this is Nathan."

Carly held out her hand in a businesslike way, and Nathan shook it, looking up at her with solemn, luminous eyes.

"Hello," he said.

Again Carly had that peculiar sensation of déjà vu that she'd had in the garden. She could have sworn she'd met Nathan before. "Hi," she replied, smiling.

He crinkled his nose. "Mom said you were a queen. I thought you'd be wearing a bathing suit and a crown," he informed her.

Carly laughed. "I'm a reporter," she said, spreading her hands. "No queens around here."

Once Mark had hustled them out the door, they drove to Fisherman's Wharf in Helen's sedate Mercedes and watched the street performers. There were mimes and banjo players and even acrobats, all combining to give the place the festive flavor of a medieval fair.

Carly busied herself exploring the little shops for an hour or so, while Mark and Nathan sat quietly on a bench, talking. Occasionally she checked on them, and it twisted her heart that the expressions on their faces were so serious.

Having no real idea what ten-year-old boys liked, Carly selected a deck of trick cards in a magic shop, along with a bottle of disappearing ink. When Mark and Nathan had had an hour to talk, she joined them.

To her relief, they looked delighted to see her.

"I'm hungry," Nathan announced.

Mark glanced at Carly in question, and she shook her head. She was still full from lunch.

He bought hot, spicy sausages for himself and Nathan, and they ate as they explored the waterfront. When the wind off the water became chilly, they went back to the car.

"I bought you something," Carly told Nathan a little shyly, holding the bag from the magic shop out to him.

He reached between the car seats to accept the gift. "Thank you," he said politely. The bag crackled as he opened it. "Wow! *Disappearing ink!*"

Mark was pulling the expensive car into traffic. "Just don't spill it. Your grandmother wouldn't appreciate that."

Nathan gave a peal of delighted laughter. "She'd never know, Dad—it would disappear!"

They went to an adventure movie after that, and then to dinner at a rustic place on the waterfront.

By the time the evening was over, Nathan was asleep in the back seat of Helen's car, the deck of magic cards still clasped in his hand.

Just looking at him made Carly's heart swell inside her until it seemed to fill her whole chest.

Mark brought the car to a stop in front of a town house on a steep, winding street, and Jeanine appeared on the porch as he awakened his son. "Come on, Buddy," he said quietly. "It's time to hit the sack."

Nathan woke up slowly and gave Carly a sleepy grin. "Would you sign my cast? Please?"

Carly swallowed and nodded, rummaging through her purse until she found a pen. She wrote her name beneath Pauly Tosselli's, and drew a heart beside it.

"Thanks," Nathan said. "When you come back, I'll know a whole bunch of card tricks."

"Okay," Carly replied in a small voice.

She waited in the car while Nathan and Mark approached the house. When Mark returned, his expression was strained.

She laid a hand on his arm. "It's progress, Mark. A few weeks ago Jeanine wouldn't even let you see him."

"She smells like she spent the afternoon at the bottom of a bourbon bottle," he answered tightly.

They drove back through darkened, picturesque streets that could only have belonged to one city.

"You neglected to mention," Carly ventured teasingly, her hand caressing the suede-upholstered car seat, "that your parents are rolling in money."

Mark relaxed a little and flashed her a grin. "Darn. I was going to tell you I'd started as a lowly paperboy."

"Is this the old stuff, or are you *nouveau riche?*"

"It's been around a few generations—my great-great-grandfather was a forty-eighter."

"A what?"

"He got here a year before the other guys."

Carly laughed. "And a hundred and forty-two years later you're still carrying on the tradition," she said.

Mark's grin broadened and took on a cocky air. "Yeah."

When they reached the Holbrooks' house, Mark's father was home. He was an imposing man with a full head of snow-white hair, a ready smile and a firm handshake.

"So this is the reporter I've heard so much about," he said, winning Carly's heart with a single sentence. "It's about time my son had a little competition."

The four of them had nightcaps together and talked, and then Carly excused herself, wanting to give Mark and his parents some private time.

She almost jumped out of her skin when she came out of the guest bathroom, freshly showered and dressed in an oversize T-shirt, to find Mark sitting cross-legged in the middle of her bed. He was wearing a pair of black-and-gray striped pajama bottoms and nothing else.

"Eleanor laid them out for me," he said a little defensively when Carly giggled. "The least I could do was wear them."

"Get off my bed, Mr. Holbrook."

He fell back against the pillows, pretending to pull at an arrow lodged in his chest, and when Carly bent over him to repeat her order, he grabbed her and flung her down on the mattress beside him.

Her squirming struggles ended, as usual, when he kissed her. She wrapped her arms around his neck and scooted close to him.

Presently he tore his mouth from hers, his eyes dancing. Rising off the bed, he pulled Carly with him and led her toward the inner door, one finger to his lips.

His room was shadowy, but she could make out pennants on the walls, and framed pictures of athletes. "Do you know how long I've fantasized about this?" he whispered.

"What?"

He set her down on the edge of the bed and bent to subdue her with another kiss. "This," he finally answered long moments later when she was rummy and disoriented. "Sneaking a girl into my room."

Carly giggled. "Come on. You don't expect me to believe you never tried that!"

"I tried, and my mother, Helen the Terrible, always caught me. She'd rap on the door and say, 'This is a raid.' It always threw cold water on the moment, if you know what I mean."

Despite their bantering, Carly was trembling with excitement. She sighed when Mark laid her back on the mattress and began raising the T-shirt. Finally he pulled it off over her head, and she lay before him, naked except for a mantle of shimmering moonlight. Her nipples tightened and flushed dark rose under his perusal.

"You're so beautiful, Carly," he said, his voice low and husky. His hand came to rest lightly on her belly. "So remarkably beautiful."

She reached up and clasped her hands behind his head. "Come here and kiss me," she said, and drew him down to her mouth.

He moved his hands in ever-broadening circles. With his fingers he explored her satiny thighs, then parted them to venture into the tangle of silk.

Carly tried to wriggle farther onto the mattress, but Mark wouldn't let her. He kissed his way down her body until he was kneeling beside the bed, the undersides of her knees clasped gently in his hands.

"I can't be quiet," she choked out in a panic. "Not if you do that."

"Then don't be quiet," he answered, and Carly pressed the corner of a pillow against her mouth to stifle her involuntary cry when he took her into his mouth.

She tossed her head from side to side as he enjoyed her, and she bit down on her lower lip to keep the noise to a minimum.

Mark was ruthless. He brought Carly to an excruciating release that arched her back like a swan's neck, his hands fondling her breasts as she whimpered, swamped in pleasure, unable to stop the violent spasms of her body.

Finally she collapsed to the mattress, gasping for breath, her skin glistening with perspiration.

Mark wouldn't let her rest. Seated on the floor now, with his back to the bed, he made her stand over him while he teased and tempted her, always stopping just short of appeasing her.

When she pleaded in broken gasps, he laid her down and came into her in a long, gliding thrust. After a few measured strokes, Carly's feeble control snapped. She hurled her body upward to meet his as a resonant string was plucked deep inside her, its single note shuddering throughout her body.

But her greatest satisfaction was in hearing Mark groan as her flesh consumed his, drawing on him with primitive greed. He was made to give everything.

"Are you using anything?" he gasped a full fifteen minutes later when they were both coming out of their dazes.

Carly laughed. "Now's a nice time to think about that, Holbrook. I love it when the man takes responsibility."

He lifted his head from her breast, and the moonlight caught something strange and somber in his eyes.

"It's okay," she said softly, entangling her fingers in his hair. "I bought something while we were out."

"Carly." The name came out as a rasp.

She stroked the sides of his face. Maybe he hadn't made up his mind what he felt, but she knew her side of things. She was desperately in love. "What?"

"If I asked you to, would you give me a baby?"

Carly gazed up at him for a long time before she answered. "That depends on whether you planned to walk off with the little dickens or let me have a hand in raising it."

"We'd raise it together."

She sighed. "How do we know we wouldn't want to break up in six months or six years?"

"How does anybody know that, Carly? If everybody had demanded a guarantee, the human race would have died out before the dinosaurs did."

"I'd need some promises from you, Mark. Some pretty heavy-duty ones."

He lowered his head to her breast and circled the nipple with his tongue, causing it to jut out in renewed response. "How's this one, Scoop? As long as you want me, I'll be around."

Carly's eyes were wet. "This is scary," she said. "A month ago I was minding my own business, getting ready to come out here and start a new job.

I'd never met the man who could get past my defenses. Now all of a sudden I'm lying in bed with you and talking babies."

Mark raised himself to look into her face, and kissed away her tears. "I know what you mean," he said, his voice a gentle rasp. "It's kind of like being caught in an avalanche."

Carly's laughter caught on a sob. "Such tender, romantic words."

Just then there was a light knock at the door.

"It's a raid!" Mark whispered, and jerked the covers up over Carly's head.

"Good night, son," his father called from the hallway.

7

The Holbrooks held an impromptu brunch the next day, and Carly was surprised at the variety of people who attended on such short notice. Mark introduced her to a bank president, a congressman and a film agent before she'd even finished her orange juice.

When Jeanine arrived, he excused himself and approached his ex-wife. Carly knew he was going to ask for custody of Nathan, and she crossed her fingers for him and stepped out onto the terrace to look at the Bay. The fainter blue of the sky and the deep navy of the water blended into azure at the horizon, and Carly yearned to hide the sight in her heart and carry it away with her.

"Lovely, isn't it?"

Carly turned, a little startled, to see Edina Peters, the film agent. "Yes," she said. "I could look at it forever."

Ms. Peters, a petite, well-dressed woman in her mid-forties, smiled, the spring sun glinting in her bright brown hair. "Who knows? Maybe you lived here in another life and were very happy. That would account—at least in part—for that look of controlled sorrow I see in your face."

Pushing a lock of windblown hair back from her forehead, Carly changed the subject. "Have you known the Holbrooks long?"

"Yes," she answered simply.

Carly was never sure, when she looked back on that moment, what made her say what she did then. "Mark wrote a play, and it's fabulous."

Edina's interest was obviously piqued. "I'm not surprised. After all, he has achieved a certain amount of success. Did he ever tell you that he was writing potboilers for detective and science-fiction magazines before he was even out of high school?"

Carly smiled and shook her head. She could easily picture Mark in that room where he'd made love to her, hurriedly penning stories on a yellow legal pad. "He's remarkable."

"Is he going to show the play to anyone?" Edina asked carefully.

Still leaning against the terrace railing, Carly interlocked her fingers and sighed. "He gave it to me," she said.

"*Gave* it to you?"

Carly shrugged, drinking in the view, taking solace in it. "I wouldn't put my name on it, or anything like that."

"Of course not," agreed Edina, who had no way of knowing what Carly's scruples were.

"I'd like to show it to someone, just to find out whether or not my instincts are right. Would you be willing...?"

Except for a glint in Edina's eyes, there was no outward sign of her eagerness. "I'd be happy to. And, naturally, I wouldn't do anything without talking to you first."

Carly nodded, went upstairs by the back way and took the manuscript from her suitcase. Edina was waiting in the kitchen when she came down, and her slender white hand trembled slightly as she reached for the play.

"Now remember," Carly said firmly, "I'm only looking for your opinion. I don't have the authority to sell Mark's work."

Edina nodded, gave Carly her card and left the party five minutes later.

Carly returned to the brunch to find that Mark had finished his talk with Jeanine. She knew it hadn't gone well by the strained look in his eyes and the muscle that kept bunching along his jawline.

She slipped her arm through his and pulled him into an alcove. "Well?"

"She said no."

Carly reached up to still the angry muscle. "You didn't really expect her to say yes so easily, did you? Good heavens, Mark, Nathan is her *son.*"

He let out a ragged sigh. "Jeanine's an alcoholic," he said.

"That doesn't mean she doesn't love her child," Carly reasoned. "What you're asking is the hardest thing in the world for a woman to do." She thought fleetingly of the play, and felt an ache inside—and an urge to run after Edina Peters and ask her to give the manuscript back.

Mark pushed back the sleeve of his forest-green sweater and checked his watch. "We've got to catch a plane in two hours, Scoop," he said in a lighter tone. "Maybe we'd better start inching toward the door."

Carly stood on her toes to kiss his cheek. "It's so nice of you to keep me advised of our schedule," she mocked with a twinkle in her eyes. "First you tell me we're coming down here because of the piece on fathers' rights, without giving me any idea of how long we're staying, then you present me to your family, then you calmly announce that we're leaving in two hours. Is there anything else I should know, Mr. Holbrook?"

He leaned toward her and grinned, lifting his eyebrows a degree. "Yeah. You should know that when we get back to Oregon, I'm going to take you to bed and make love to you until you collapse in exhaustion.''

A blush colored Carly's cheeks, and she turned away, infuriated that he could arouse her so thoroughly in a room full of people, then leave her to wait hours for satisfaction.

Forty-five minutes later, after Mark had spent a little more time with Nathan, he and Carly said goodbye to his family, got into a cab and headed for the airport.

The fact that she'd given the play to an agent was preying on Carly's conscience by then, but she didn't have the courage to confide in Mark. She pushed the subject to the back of her mind and the two of them brainstormed the fathers' rights issue during the flight back to Oregon.

"Are you coming home with me?" Mark asked as they landed.

Carly twisted the exquisite gold bracelet on her wrist. "No," she said after nervously running the tip of her tongue over her lips. "I think we need some space."

He didn't comment on that until they were out of the plane and on the way to the baggage-claim area.

"What's going on, Carly?" he demanded as they rode the escalator. "I thought things were pretty good between us."

Carly felt sad. "They are," she answered. "But they're volatile, too. I don't want this relationship to go up like a bomb and crash to the ground in flaming pieces, and it could if we push too hard."

He gave her a weary grin. "I hate to admit it, Scoop, but you may be right. But *damn,* I really wanted to make love to you tonight."

Again Carly blushed. "Well—you could come to my apartment for dinner. It's just that I don't think we should live together. Not yet."

His brown eyes caressed her. "Fair enough, but what about that baby we talked about?"

Carly glanced anxiously around to see if anyone was eavesdropping on their conversation. "I think we should forget that, at least until after this thing about Nathan's custody is ironed out. Creating a child isn't something you do on impulse, Mark, and besides…" She paused, swallowed and averted her eyes for a few moments before going on. "You can't replace one child with another."

He sighed, slipped an arm around her waist and pulled her close against his side. "All right, Scoop, you win. But we can at least *practice,* so that when we do make a baby, we'll get it right."

Carly laughed, but inside her there was a great sadness. For all her sensible decisions, what she really wanted was to pack up everything she owned, move into Mark's house and start a baby right away.

What she *didn't* want was to end up divorced in a few years because they'd tried to do things too quickly.

After collecting their baggage, Carly and Mark drove to his place. Carly waited in the car while he collected his portable computer and a change of clothes. They stopped briefly at a Chinese restaurant, then retreated to Carly's apartment.

The light on her answering machine was flickering, and Carly had already pushed the button and started the tape playing before she realized there might be messages she didn't want Mark to hear.

Sure enough, Janet's voice filled the living room. "I'll bet you're off in some romantic hideaway with that fantastic man you're dating, you fink. Call me when you get back."

Mark, who was sitting on the couch, opening the bags from the Chinese place, paused long enough to polish his fingernails against his shirt and toss Carly a cocky grin.

Subtly she went back to the machine and pressed the Off button. Then she kicked off her shoes and curled up beside Mark on the cushions. They watched an old movie on TV while they ate casually from the cartons, occasionally feeding each other, and the progression to the bedroom was a natural one.

Carly went in to change her clothes, and in the ancient way of men, Mark followed her.

"Remember what I told you in San Francisco?" he teased, his voice a low, throaty rumble as he stood behind her, his lips moving against her nape.

In spite of herself, Carly trembled. His words hadn't been far out of her mind since he'd spoken them. "Yes," she managed as he lifted her tank top and closed his hands over the bare, full breasts beneath.

He nipped at her earlobe. "What did I say?"

Carly wondered if there were other women in the world who'd gone from virgin to vamp in one easy lesson. "Y-you said you were going to t-take me to bed and make love to me until I c-collapsed."

Mark turned her in his arms and pulled the tank top off over her head. Her plump breasts bobbed with the motion, and two patches of color throbbed in her cheeks. He lifted her up, and she wrapped her legs around his waist, her arms encircling his neck.

He was kissing her collarbone, the warm, quivering tops of her breasts. He found her nipple and suckled, and she flung back her head in ecstatic surrender, pulling in her breath. His glossy brown hair was like silk between her fingers.

"Tell me what you want, Carly," he paused to mutter.

"You," Carly answered in a helpless whisper. "On top of me, inside me—part of me . . ."

Mark laid her down on the bed and pulled away the shorts and panties she'd just put on. His eyes glittered with desire as he entered her.

Their time together was everything it had ever been, and more. Carly thought, at times, that she could not endure the pleasure, that she would be unable to survive it. When the tumult had overtaken them, when glory had been reached and shared, they lay quietly for a long time, shadows slipping over them. And Carly wept.

"What?" Mark asked gruffly, brushing away her tears with his thumbs.

"I want this to work," Carly managed to respond, feeling silly and bereft. "I want so much for this to work."

Mark kissed her, not in a demanding way, but in a gentle, reassuring one. Then he got up and held out his hand to her. "That part of it is up to us, Scoop—it's not like we're at the mercy of a whimsical fate or anything."

He led her to the bathroom and they showered together, then Mark dried himself with a towel and began putting his clothes back on. Carly, wearing her pink robe, stood in the doorway, watching him, thinking what a marvel he was. His body was beautifully sculpted, like one of Michelangelo's statues come to life.

"You're leaving?" she asked softly.

He paused in the hunt for his other shoe long enough to plant a kiss on her forehead. "Yes. You're all done in, babe. You need some rest."

Carly swallowed. "I guess loving you is exhausting work," she said.

Mark stopped and recoiled comically, like a victim in one of the old Frankenstein movies. "Did I actually hear it? The L word?"

Carly nodded. It was so hard, taking the risk, laying all her feelings on the line when he might just walk out and never come back. "I love you, Mark."

He came to her, gripped her shoulders gently in his hands and searched her face. "Carly, I'm going to owe half of next year's income when I say this, because I bet all my friends I'd never let it happen, but I love you, too. And it's not like anything I've ever felt before."

She was too moved to speak, so she just nodded again, and he kissed her lightly and went back to the search for his shoe.

"Get some shut-eye, Scoop," he said. "Tomorrow we start working in earnest." After that, he kissed her once more and left.

Carly locked the apartment door after him and let her forehead rest against the wood.

Presently she turned around and made her way to the desk. A series of messages played while she gathered up the cartons and bags left on the coffee table from their Chinese meal. Abruptly she stiffened when Edina's voice filled the room.

"Carly, you were right—this play is wonderful. I read it at one sitting. We've simply *got* to persuade Mark to let me market it. Call me back at the number I gave you on Monday morning, and we'll formulate a plan."

Carly's knees weakened as she imagined what would have happened if she hadn't turned off the machine after Janet's message played. She dropped the debris from dinner into the trash and made her way somewhat shakily to the telephone.

Janet answered on the third ring.

"It's me," Carly said, and then she began to cry.

Her friend was there in less than a minute. "What's wrong?" she asked, taking in Carly's mussed hair, bathrobe and tear-reddened eyes.

"I'm in love with Mark!" Carly wailed.

Janet smiled gently as she pressed her friend into a chair and then went to the kitchenette, talking loudly to be heard over the sound of water running into the teapot. "Now there's stunning news," she called. "Nobody would have guessed you were crazy about the guy or anything."

Carly got out of the chair and followed her friend's voice, watching as Janet took mugs and tea bags from their respective places. "I've done something sneaky and underhanded," she went on, sniffling. "He's probably never going to forgive me."

Arms folded, Janet leaned against the kitchen counter to wait for the water to boil and sighed. "What could you have done that was so bad?" she asked skeptically.

Carly bit her lower lip for a long moment before answering. "I showed his play to an agent without telling him first."

Janet's pretty eyes went round. "You did what?"

"It seemed like a good idea at the time," Carly reasoned fitfully. "And I told the agent I didn't have the power to sell it. But she called back a little while ago—it was just lucky that Mark didn't hear the message—and I have an awful feeling she's not going to be able to control her enthusiasm."

The teakettle whistled, and Janet poured boiling water into the two mugs and carried them past Carly to the table, where they both sat down.

"You're right," Janet said. "I think you're in very big trouble."

Carly nodded miserably, her fingers curved around the steaming mug. "I thought it would be okay," she said. "I mean, he *said* I could do what I wanted to with it, and his mother and I tacitly agreed that somebody in the business ought to look at it. That might even have been why she invited Edina to the brunch."

Janet didn't pursue the subject of the Holbrooks' brunch. "You've got to tell Mark what you did before he hears it from somebody else," she said. "It's your only chance, Carly. If the agent calls him and starts raving about what a hit the movie's going to be, he'll be furious with you."

Carly's throat ached, and she was on the verge of tears again. "Do you suppose I did this on purpose, Janet? You know, to sabotage myself, to keep things from being too good?"

"You've been watching too much trash TV," Janet said, dismissing the idea with a wave of one hand. "You did it because you love the man, and you want to see him get the recognition he deserves. Thing is, your methods leave something to be desired, kid."

Mark's portable computer was still sitting on the coffee table—they'd never gotten around to actually using it—and the sight filled Carly with guilt. With shaking hands, she lifted the mug full of tea to her mouth.

"He'll probably be mad at first," Janet went on when Carly didn't speak. "But he'll see that you meant well when he calms down."

Remembering how Mark had exploded when she'd confessed that she'd *read* the play, Carly had her doubts about what his reactions would be when he learned she'd shown it to someone else. Now, she guessed, she'd see how much—or how little—Mark loved her. She grimaced.

"There's always the sneaky way out," Janet suggested. "You could call the agent, tell her to send back the play and never breathe a word about it to anybody—after which you conveniently forget to mention the blunder to Mark."

Carly dismissed the idea with a shake of her head and, "I'd never have a moment's peace for worrying that he'd find out."

Janet gestured toward the phone. "Call him. I'll be down the hall if you need me." With that she got out of her chair, carried her cup to the sink and then left the apartment.

Carly stared after her, her thumbnail caught between her front teeth, but she didn't make the call. No, she reasoned, she wouldn't do that until after she'd spoken to Edina in the morning and asked her to send the play back.

She made herself another cup of tea, selected a book from the shelves underneath the living room window and went to bed. It seemed lonely without Mark.

Fluffing her pillows behind her, Carly opened the new adventure-espionage novel she'd bought at the grocery store and began to read. By the time she'd gone over the same paragraph for the third time, she gave up.

There were dark circles under her eyes when she got up the next morning, and no matter how skillful she was with her makeup, she couldn't hide them. She had tried Edina's office number twice, without success, when Mark showed up.

The moment he got a look at her face, he frowned and put a hand to her forehead. "You're not looking so good, Scoop. Are you sick?"

Yes, Carly thought miserably. "No," she said out loud.

He didn't look convinced. "I can start the interviews without you," he said. "And I'll bring my notes by later, so we can go over them."

"Mark, I'm new on this job. I don't want to mess up—"

"One day won't make a difference, Carly. And, like I said, I can get the legwork done without you."

Stubbornly Carly shook her head. She grabbed an orange while Mark reached for the portable computer, and they set out to begin their day's work. It was ten o'clock before she got a chance to sneak out of Mark's office at the *Times*, where they'd been arranging interviews with divorced fathers, and put a call through to Edina.

"Did you talk to Mark?" the agent asked immediately.

Carly sat on the corner of her desk, the telephone receiver pressed to her ear. "No," she said. "I shouldn't have given you the play without talking to Mark first. I want you to send it back."

There was a short, stunned silence on the other end of the line. "Ms. Barnett, this is a very special property, and I could have half a dozen producers fighting over it by nightfall."

"I just wanted your opinion, remember?" Carly said, pulling her reading glasses off and setting them aside on the desk with a clatter. "Please. Just express it back to me—"

"I can't do that, I'm afraid. I'm going to call Mark myself. We're old friends—maybe he'll listen to reason."

Carly fairly leaped off the desk. "You can't do that," she cried in a frantic whisper. "He'll be furious—"

Edina sighed indulgently. "Mark is quick-tempered, I'll give you that. But once he's had time to think—"

"Send back the manuscript!" Carly broke in.

"If Mark asks me to—personally—I will."

Rage and panic filled Carly as the door of her office opened and Mark peered around it. "Ready to go out and talk to the man in the street?" he asked.

"Goodbye," Carly said into the receiver, and slammed it down.

Mark's eyebrows drew together in a frown. "Who was that?"

Carly tried to smile, and failed. She wanted to tell Mark the truth, but she was afraid.

They went back to work after that, and for the next three days, they were busy. By the time Mark was ready to draft the first version of the article, Carly was sure they'd talked to every divorced father in Portland.

Mark worked on the computer on his desk at home, and the keys clicked rapidly as his fingers raced to keep up with his thoughts. Carly stood behind him, one hand resting on his shoulder, reading the little green words as fast as they appeared on the screen.

"Biased," she commented, when he finally reared back in his chair and pushed the Print button. "Some of these guys are card-carrying sewer rats and you know it. I could go to their wives and get an entirely different story!"

Mark turned far enough in his chair to give Carly a challenging look. "So do it," he said.

Carly pulled her notebook from her purse and reached for the phone. "Okay, I will," she replied, already punching out a number. She'd have to do some investigating to reach most of the ex-wives of the men she and Mark had interviewed, but she had information on a few.

When Carly arrived home late the following night, Janet brought her an express package that had been left with her by the building manager. Carly opened it right there in the hallway and found Mark's play inside.

Unconsciously she raised one hand to her heart in a gesture of relief.

Janet looked horrified. "You mean you haven't told him?"

"We've been so busy with the assignment—"

"Thin ice," Janet said as Carly left her to walk down the hallway to her own door. "You're walking on thin ice."

In the privacy of her own apartment, Carly stood holding the manuscript, her lower lip caught between her teeth. Despite everything she'd said about telling Mark, Edina had returned the play. That meant she'd changed her mind—didn't it?

She laid the play down on the table and went to the desk. As usual, the answering machine light was flickering. Carly pressed the button, steeling herself against an angry call from Mark or some kind of threat from Edina, but all the messages were from women she'd been trying to reach for interviews.

In calling them back and taking notes, Carly was able to forget her outstanding problem for a while. She wrote rapidly, nodding to herself as the divorced mothers told stories about the former husbands she and Mark had interviewed about fathers' rights.

Late that night when she'd roughed in the outline for the first draft of her article, Carly held Mark's play in both hands for a moment, then dropped it into her desk drawer. *Out of sight, out of mind,* she thought with a pang of guilt.

She spent the next day interviewing, and the day after that squirreled away in her office, writing. She had just turned the finished product, an article rebutting Mark's, in to Allison when she was called to Mr. Clark's office.

Filled with nervous excitement, Carly obeyed the summons.

After telling her to sit, Mr. Clark launched right into the assignment. There was a new shelter for battered women opening in the city, and the director had some innovative ideas. He wanted Carly to get an interview.

Carly fairly danced out of his office. Here was her chance to really show what she could do. *Carly*

Barnett, girl reporter, she thought with a happy grin. She stopped by Emmeline's desk.

"Is Mark—Mr. Holbrook in yet?"

Emmeline shook her head, seemingly unconcerned. "His hours are flexible," she said. "He pretty much sets them himself."

Carly sighed and nodded, then vanished into her office. She had work to do.

Mark stood gripping the telephone receiver, a glass of orange juice in his free hand, his body rigid with shock.

"So you see," Edina Peters finished up, "I really think it's time you stopped hiding this jewel of a play in your desk drawer and let me sell it. It could be adapted for the screen in five minutes, and we're talking major money here, Mark."

His muscles finally thawed, and he flung the orange juice at the fireplace. Glass shattered against brick. But his voice was deadly calm. "Carly showed you the play," he said like a robot, even though Edina had already told him that. He guessed he was hoping the agent would say no, she'd made a mistake, it had been someone else.

"She meant well," Edina said. "Afterwards she had an attack of conscience and begged me to send it back to her. I did—after making a few copies."

Mark closed his eyes tightly. His stomach twisted inside him, and an ache pounded at his nape. *Carly,* he thought, and the name splintered against his spirit the way the glass had against the fireplace.

"Mark?" Edina prompted.

He felt sick. He forced himself to speak evenly, to relax his grip on the receiver. "I'm here, Edina," he rasped.

"Will you let me sell it?"

My guts are in that play, he thought. *It's an open door to my soul.* "No," he answered.

"But—"

"The discussion is over," he broke in. And then he hung up the telephone with only a moderate crash.

He'd planned to work at home that day on a human-interest piece he and Clark had been discussing, but now that he knew what Carly had done, he could only think of one thing—confronting her. Resolute, he strode into the bathroom, stripped off the shorts and T-shirt he'd worn for a late-morning run and showered.

He dressed hastily, and drove away from the house with his tires screeching on the asphalt. He shouldn't have trusted Carly, he thought as he sped down the freeway. He shouldn't have loved her.

He jammed one hand through his hair and cursed when he heard a siren behind him, then glanced into his rearview mirror. A silver-blue light whirled on top of the squad car—sure enough, he was the man the officer wanted to see.

Filled with quiet rage, Mark pulled over to the side of the road and waited.

8

Carly had been down in the morgue in the basement of the newspaper building, reading up on past articles about shelters for battered women, and her heart did a little leap when the doors whisked open in the lobby to reveal Mark.

Her instant smile faded when their eyes linked, however, and she knew in that moment that she'd waited too long to tell him about the play. She wanted to explain, but when she tried to speak, no sound came out of her mouth.

Mark jabbed a button on the panel and the doors closed. The look in his eyes was cold and remote. "I guess I didn't lose those bets with my buddies after all," he said, his voice as rough as gravel in a rusty can. "I wasn't in love—just lust."

Carly sagged against the wall of the elevator, her hands gripping the stainless-steel railing. "That was cruel," she said. "I had a reason for what I did."

He struck another button, and the elevator stopped where it was. His hands came to rest against the wall on either side of Carly's head, and his eyes bored into hers. "Oh?" he rasped.

She swallowed, wanting to duck beneath his arm and start the elevator going again, but unable to move. She was like a sparrow gazing into the eyes of a cobra. "I wanted a professional opinion," she managed to say. "I was h-hoping to persuade you to let *Broken Vows* be produced."

Mark ran the tip of one index finger down the V of her blouse in a impudent caress. "And make lots of money? The joke's on you, baby—I already have a fortune. And until an hour ago I would have given you anything you wanted."

Carly's eyes stung with tears of humiliation and frustration. "Will you stop being a melodramatic bastard and listen to me, please? I don't give a damn about your money—I never did! I wanted to see the play produced because something that good should be—"

"Shared with the world?" he interrupted acidly, arching one eyebrow. "Come on, Carly—that's a cliché."

"I'm not the one who said it," she pointed out, battling for composure. "You did."

He turned away, touched another button and set the elevator moving again. "Goodbye, Carly," he said. His broad shoulders barred her from him like a high, impenetrable wall, and when the doors opened on their floor, he stepped out.

Carly couldn't move, she was so filled with pain. And she let the elevator go all the way back to the lobby before she pressed the proper button. Reaching her floor, she hurried into her office, glancing neither right nor left, and closed the door.

She was sitting behind her desk, still trying to pull herself together, when Emmeline buzzed her and announced, with a question in her voice, that Helen Holbrook was on the line.

"Hello, Helen," Carly greeted Mark's mother sadly, not knowing what to expect. Despite their conversation in the garden that day in San Francisco, the woman was probably furious with her, and Carly steeled herself to be harangued.

"Edina told me about the play," Helen said, her voice calm. "She said Mark wasn't pleased that you'd shown it to her."

Recalling the way he'd looked at her in the elevator, the cold, bitter way he'd spoken, Carly was anguished. "I'd say that was an understatement," she got out. "He doesn't want to have anything to do with me now."

Helen sighed. "Mark can be positively insufferable. He's hardheaded, just like his father."

A despairing smile tugged at the corners of Carly's mouth. "You're being very kind," she said, "but there's something else you're trying to tell me, isn't there?"

"Yes," Helen confessed in a rush. "Carly, something has happened, and I don't want Mark to be told about it over the telephone. I must ask you to talk to him for me."

Images of another automobile accident, with Nathan seriously hurt, filled Carly's mind with garish sounds and colors. "What is it?" she whispered.

"Jeanine has crashed her car again," Helen said sadly. "Nathan wasn't with her, thank God, but naturally he's very upset."

Carly's forehead was resting in her hand. "And Jeanine?"

"She's in a coma, Carly, and not expected to live."

Carly squeezed her eyes closed, remembering the beautiful auburn-haired woman who had once been Mark's wife. "My God."

"Jeanine has her parents, but Nathan needs Mark. Carly, could you please go to him and tell him, as gently as you can, what's happened?"

After swallowing hard, she nodded and said, "Yes." Her heart twisted inside her to think how frightened Nathan must be. "Yes, Helen, I'll tell him."

"Thank you," Helen replied with tears in her voice. Then she added, "I'll try to reason with Mark while he's here. He loves you, and he's an idiot if he throws away what you've got together."

Carly thought of the look she'd seen in Mark's eyes and grieved. She knew that as far as he was concerned, their relationship was over. "Thanks," she said softly. Then the two women said their goodbyes and hung up.

Carly found Mark in his office, standing at the window and glaring out at the city. His name sounded hoarse when she said it.

He turned to glower at her.

"Mark, there's been an accident," she said in measured tones. She saw the fear leap in his eyes and added quickly, "Nathan wasn't hurt—it's Jeanine. She's—she's not expected to live."

The color drained out of Mark's face, and Carly longed to put her arms around him, but she didn't dare. In his mood, he would probably push her away, and she knew she couldn't bear that. "Dear God," he said, and turned around to punch out a number on his telephone.

Carly slipped out of the office and closed the door.

Mark left five minutes later without saying goodbye, and Carly went into the women's rest room and splashed cold water on her face until she was sure she wouldn't cry. Then she went back to work.

When quitting time came, the relief was almost overwhelming. She stuffed her files and notes into her briefcase, snatched up her purse and drove home in a daze. When she pulled into her parking space in the apartment lot, she was ashamed to realize the drive had passed without her noticing.

She went to her apartment without stopping for the mail or a word with Janet, dropped all her things just inside the door and then raced into her room, flung herself down on the bed and sobbed.

After a while, though, she began to think that if Mark was so easily angered, so lacking in understanding or compassion, she didn't want him anyway.

At least, that was what she told herself. Inside, she felt raw and broken, as though a part of her had been torn away. Carly showered, put on shorts and a summer top and went downstairs to exercise.

When she got back to her apartment, the phone was ringing. Carly made a lunge for it and gasped out an anxious hello, praying the caller was Mark. That he'd come to his senses.

She was both disappointed and relieved to hear her father's voice. "Hello, Carly."

Instantly Carly wanted to start blubbering again, but she held herself in check. Her dad was hundreds of miles away, and there was nothing to be gained by dragging him into her problems. "Hi, Dad. What's up?"

"I just thought I'd tell you that I liked that piece you sent me about the food contest. That was really good reporting."

In spite of everything, Carly had to smile. Don Barnett wasn't interested in soufflés and coffee cakes, she knew that. He called purely because he cared. "Thanks, Dad. I'm expecting a Pulitzer at the very least."

He chuckled. "I never was very good at coming up with excuses. I want to know what's the matter, and don't you dare say 'nothing.'"

Carly let out a ragged sigh. "I finally fell head over heels and it didn't work out."

"What do you mean, it didn't work out?" her dad demanded. "What kind of lamebrain would throw away a chance to make a life with you?"

"One named Mark Holbrook."

"Is there anything I can do?"

"Yeah," Carly answered, making a joke to keep from crying. "You can eat a banana split in my honor. I'd like to drown my sorrows in junk food, but if I do, none of my clothes will fit."

"Maybe you should just get on a plane and come back here, sweetheart. Ryerton may not be a metropolis, but we do have a newspaper."

Carly was already shaking her head. "No way, Dad—I'm standing my ground. I have as much right to live in Portland and work at the *Times* as Mark does."

"Okay, then I'll come out there. I'll black his eyes for him."

Carly smiled at the images that came to her mind, then remembered that Jeanine was lying in a hospital, near death, and was solemn again. "I'm okay," she insisted. "If you want to come out and visit, terrific. But you're not blacking anybody's eyes."

"Maybe I'll do that. Maybe I'll just get on an airplane and come out there."

"That would be great, Dad," Carly said, knowing her father wouldn't leave Kansas except under the most dire circumstances. He hadn't been on a plane in twenty years.

Five minutes later, when Carly hung up, she dialed the Holbrooks' number in San Francisco, and Mark's father answered.

"Hello," he said when she'd introduced herself, and there was a cool note in his voice.

Carly wondered what Mark had told him about her. "I'm sorry to bother you, but I wanted to know if there was any news about Jeanine."

Mr. Holbrook sighed. "She's taken a turn for the better," he said. "The doctors are pretty sure she'll survive, though how long it will take her to recover completely is anybody's guess." His voice was a degree or two warmer now. "Shall I ask Mark to call you when he comes in, Carly?"

She shook her head, forgetting for a moment that Mr. Holbrook couldn't see her. "No!" she said too quickly. She paused, cleared her throat and tried to speak in a more moderate tone. "Please don't mention me to Mark at all."

"But—"

"Please, Mr. Holbrook. It will only upset him, and he needs to be able to concentrate on helping Nathan right now."

Mark's father didn't agree or disagree; he simply asked Carly to take care of herself and said goodbye.

Jeanine was lying in the intensive care unit, tubes running into her bruised and battered body, her head bandaged. She opened her eyes when Mark took her hand, and her fingers tightened around his.

"Nathan . . . ?" she managed to rasp.

"He's safe, Jeanine."

Tears formed in the corners of her eyes. "Are you—taking him home?"

It wouldn't be a kindness to lie to her, Mark decided. Jeanine needed to know their son would be loved and taken care of. "Yes," he said, still holding her hand. He didn't love her—since his relationship with Carly he'd come to realize that he never had—but it hurt him to see her suffering.

"I was drinking," she said clearly, her eyes pleading with Mark to understand.

He nodded. "You need some help, Jeanine."

She tried to smile. "Maybe it's hopeless."

Mark shook his head. "You'll make it," he said hoarsely, even though he had no idea whether that was true or not. Jeanine was in serious trouble, and they both knew it.

"Take care of Nathan," she finished. And then her eyes drifted closed and she slept.

Mark went out into the hallway to find Jeanine's father and mother waiting. They both had deep shadows under their eyes.

"Was she upset that you're taking Nathan?" his former mother-in-law asked.

Mark shook his head. "She knows I love him," he said, pitying these people, wanting to ease their pain but not knowing how. "I'm sorry you have to go through this."

The Martins nodded in weary unison, and Mark left them to keep their vigil.

When he arrived at his parents' home, his mother was waiting up for him. She served him a cup of decaffeinated coffee and launched right into her lecture. "You're a fool, Mark Holbrook. An absolute idiot."

He sighed and rubbed his tired, burning eyes with a thumb and forefinger. "Mother, I'm not in the mood for this."

"I don't care what you're in the mood for," Helen retorted. "Carly showed Edina that play because she hoped some professional feedback would convince you to let it be produced, and for no other reason."

Mark had been cherishing secret dreams of leaving the newspaper business to write plays for over a year, but he hadn't meant for *Broken Vows* to be seen by anyone. He'd written it in an attempt to clear his mind of the pain. "When I was married to Jeanine," he said slowly, "I didn't know where she was or what she was up to half the time. As you already know, I had some pretty unpleasant surprises. I don't want to live like that again."

"Carly is nothing like Jeanine, and in your heart, you know that. Besides, I believe you love her."

Mark sighed. He was tired, and he ached from the core of his spirit out. "Carly is more like Jeanine than you'd like to think, Mother," he said evenly, "and as for loving her—I'll get over it."

"Will you?" Helen challenged. "Don't be so sure of that, my dear. You can't turn love on and shut it off like a faucet, you know."

He thrust himself out of his chair and bent to kiss his mother's forehead. "Give it up," he said with quiet firmness. "It's over between Carly and me."

Upstairs, Mark carefully opened the guest-room door and stepped inside. Nathan lay sprawled on the bed, arms and legs askew, his eyelids flickering as he dreamed.

Gently Mark brushed his son's hair back from his forehead. *I wanted you to come and live with me, buddy,* he told Nathan silently, speaking from his heart, *but I didn't expect it to happen like this. Honest.*

The child stirred, then opened his eyes. "Dad?" he asked on a long yawn.

Mark sat down on the edge of the bed. "Sorry, big guy. I didn't mean to wake you up."

"Is Mom okay?"

"Yeah," Mark answered. "But she has to stay in the hospital for a while."

Nathan accepted that with the sometimes remarkable stoicism of a ten-year-old. "I can visit her, can't I?"

In that moment the decision was made. Mark would return to San Francisco, buy a town house and build a life for himself and his son. Maybe he would even write a play—one that didn't touch every raw nerve in his soul, one he could bear to show to an agent. "Sure you can visit her," he said.

"Now get some sleep. You've got school tomorrow."

Nathan screwed up his face. "I have to go to *school?*"

Mark chuckled. "No," he teased. "Of course not. A fifth-grade education will take you a long way in the world." He started to rise off the bed, but Nathan stopped him with one anxious little hand.

"Dad, where's Carly? Is she going to live with us?"

Those two simple questions left Mark feeling as though he'd just stepped into the whirling blades of a giant fan. *Carly,* he thought, and the name was a lonely cry deep in his spirit. "Carly's in Portland, doing her job," he managed to say, after a moment or two of recovery. "And no, it's just going to be the two of us for a while, buddy."

For a moment Nathan looked as though he might cry. Mark could see that the kid had been spinning dreams of a real home and a regular family in his head, and seeing his disappointment was painful. "Mom said Carly probably had a baby growing inside her. Does she, Dad?"

Mark swallowed, and it felt like he'd gulped down a petrified grapefruit. *God, I hope not,* he thought. "No," he said forcefully, trying to convince himself as well as Nathan. "No, big guy, there isn't any baby."

Emmeline looked concerned as she handed Carly her morning coffee. "I guess you know that Mr. Holbrook is leaving the paper and moving back to San Francisco," she said.

Carly felt as though Emmeline had just flung the scalding contents of the cup all over her. "N-no," she answered, avoiding the secretary's gaze and fumbling in the depths of her purse for her glasses. "No, I hadn't heard about that."

"Oh," said Emmeline, and her voice was small and confused. "I'm sorry if I said anything I shouldn't have."

Carly took her glasses from their case and poked them onto her face. "What Mr. Holbrook does is nothing to me," she lied, flipping on her computer. She'd been living at the battered women's shelter for three days, pretending to be hiding from a violent husband, and she was ready to write about the experiences of the people she'd met there.

Emmeline couldn't seem to let the subject drop. "His ex-wife was hurt in an accident, you know, and he's got custody of his son now. I guess he didn't want to uproot the kid and make it so he couldn't see his mother."

"You're probably right," Carly answered, deliberately sounding distracted and preoccupied.

Finally Emmeline took the hint. She slipped out of Carly's office with a muttered goodbye and closed the door behind her. The moment she was alone, Carly slammed one fist down on the desk and whispered, "Damn you, Holbrook. Damn you to hell."

Fortunately the article absorbed her attention for the rest of the day. As she was leaving that evening, she passed Mark's office and couldn't help noticing that Emmeline and several women from the typing pool were inside hanging streamers.

"There'll be a going-away party tomorrow," Emmeline called to her.

Carly nodded and bit her lower lip. She hadn't had to say any goodbyes to Mark; he'd said them for her. She made up her mind to busy herself outside the office the next day.

She spent a miserable night, finally falling asleep in the wee hours of the morning, only to be awakened by a wave of nausea with the rising of the sun. One hand clasped over her mouth, she made a dash for the bathroom.

"Oh, great," she complained, staggering to the kitchen for a cup of chamomile tea, "now I've got the flu."

The tea settled her stomach, though, and after a shower Carly felt better. She also felt guilty about staying away from the office just because of Mark's going-away party.

Resolutely Carly put on one of her best outfits—a pink silk suit from Hong Kong—and took extra care with her hair and makeup. She walked into the newsroom half an hour later, a Miss United States smile on her face, her briefcase swinging jauntily at her side.

When she was sure no one was watching, she fairly dived into her office and leaned against the door, feeling as though she'd just picked her way through an emotional mine field.

She switched on her computer and opened her briefcase, planning to go over her notes for a proposed article and hide out until Mark had heard a round of for-he's-a-jolly-good-fellow and left. Then Mr. Clark called an unexpected meeting.

Carly felt like a martyr being summoned from the dungeon for execution. She stood, smoothed her skirt and checked her hair and lipstick in a small mirror pulled from her purse. Then she walked bravely down the hall to the conference room.

Thanks to some cruel fate, she was seated directly across from Mark, and he was making no effort at all to ignore her. His solemn brown eyes

studied her thoughtfully while he turned an un-
sharpened pencil end over end on the tabletop.

Carly willed him to look away, and he seemed to
sense that, refusing to give in. Finally she dropped
her eyes, her cheeks burning, and devoutly wished
she'd followed her original instincts and called in
sick that day.

Mr. Clark got up and made a speech about what
an honor it had been to work with Mark Holbrook
and how they were all going to miss him. Everyone
tittered when he mentioned Mark's plans to write a
play—everyone except Carly, that is. Her eyes shot
to his face in angry question.

He responded with an infuriating grin.

After what seemed like a millennium, Mr. Clark
finished raving about Mark's accomplishments and
suggested that everyone take time for cake and
punch. Carly slipped out of the conference room
and hurried in the opposite direction.

Even in her office she could hear the laughter and
the talk, and it made her heart turn over in her
chest. Mark, gone. It was almost impossible to believe that after today she wouldn't so much as catch
a glimpse of him or hear his voice in the hallway.

She hadn't had such a hard time holding back
tears since the time she'd set the stage curtains on
fire with one of her flaming batons during the Miss

Feed and Grain pageant. She'd been fourteen then, and she felt younger than that now.

The only thing to do was work. That, her father had always told her, was the salve that healed every wound.

She turned to her computer and sat back in her chair when she saw the message flickering on her screen.

Goodbye, Scoop. Better luck next time.

That did it. Carly's tears began to flow, and she couldn't stop them. She was standing at the window, gazing out at the city and frantically drying her cheeks with a wad of tissue, when she heard a gentle rap at the door.

She was afraid to turn around—afraid Mark would be standing there, afraid he wouldn't. "Yes?"

"The party's over, Carly," Emmeline's voice said quietly. "I'll cover for you if you want to go home."

Carly was a trouper, and she knew the show had to go on, no matter what kind of show it was. But the front she was hiding behind was teetering dangerously, and she needed to be alone. She nodded without looking at the secretary, grimly amused that she'd thought no one in the office knew about her affair with Mark.

What a naive little idiot you were, she scolded herself, gathering up her purse and turning off the computer. She left her briefcase behind, under no delusion that she would get any worthwhile work done that night.

When she arrived at her apartment, she stayed only long enough to exchange her silk suit for cut-off jeans and a turquoise T-shirt. She went to a matinee at the mall, where she cried silently all through a comedy, then had supper at a fast-food place. When she still couldn't face going home after that, she went to another movie.

She never remembered what that one was about.

In the morning Mr. Clark called her into his office and asked her if she was aware that she was covered by a company health plan. "You don't look well, Ms. Barnett," he finished.

It's only a broken heart, Carly wanted to reply. *In about sixty years it will probably heal.* "I guess I'm just a little tired," she said, hoping he wouldn't decide the job was too much for her. Being demoted or getting fired would be beyond bearing.

"I liked that piece you did on battered women. It was damn good."

Carly was reassured, if only slightly. "Thank you. I've been thinking about a piece on women entrepreneurs—"

Mr. Clark waved her into silence. "No, that's been done too much lately. There's a river rafting expedition leaving on Saturday—one of those things meant to give executives confidence in their inner strength. I'd like you to go along on that. It's going to last about three days."

Carly thought of pitching through rapids and spinning in whirlpools and felt her flu symptoms returning, but she managed a brilliant smile. "That sounds exciting," she said.

"Of course, we'll send a photographer along, too. That way, if one of you drowns, the other one can still bring back the story." Mr. Clark beamed at his joke, and Carly dutifully laughed.

Carly took down the information he gave her and left the office early. She had preparations to make, and she was going to need hiking boots, flannel shirts and a sleeping bag, among other things. She went shopping and bought more things than she could possibly have carried without help from a lot of people who were willing to call her bwana.

On the way home her car mysteriously headed toward Mark's house instead of the apartment building. She knew he wasn't there as soon as she reached the end of the driveway, but she didn't leave. She just sat, her eyes brimming with tears, remembering how she and Mark had talked and laughed and made love in that house. She'd given him her virginity there, and no matter how many men she might meet in the future, she would never forget that first night in Mark's arms.

She touched the gold bracelet he'd given her, then fumbled open the catch. Stepping up onto the porch, she dropped the glimmering chain through the mail slot. Then Carly hurried back to her car, started the ignition and left.

That night she slept, but it was only because of nervous exhaustion. And in the morning she was sick again. Evidently, she decided, she'd caught some kind of intermittent flu. She made herself a cup of herbal tea, forced it down and presently felt better.

She spent the day at a local high-school gymnasium, sitting on the bleachers with a lot of other potential adventurers, listening to the head river rafter explain what was involved in the expedition. He said the trip wasn't for weaklings, and anybody who couldn't stand three measly days grappling with the wilderness should just go home and forget the whole thing.

That option sounded good to Carly, but she had her job to think about, so she stayed. Besides, she needed to stay busy in order to keep herself from dwelling on Mark and all the things that could have been.

She drove home that night and found a message from Jim Benson, the anchorman, on her machine. He obviously knew that Mark had left town, and he wanted to know if Carly would have supper with him after the six o'clock newscast.

"What the hell?" Carly said to her empty apartment. Life was like a river, and she had to raft down it. She called Jim back and left a message with his secretary that she'd meet him at the station at seven o'clock.

9

Jim's gaze was filled with gentle discernment as he joined Carly in his office after the newscast. "You're as gorgeous as ever," he said, "but you look as though somebody's been batting you around like a croquet ball."

Carly managed a smile. That 'somebody' was Mark Holbrook and they both knew it. "And this is a pity date, is that it?"

Jim chuckled and shook his head. "Nothing so magnanimous," he said. "I'm still nursing a vain hope that when you get over Mark, you'll begin to see that I'm a nice guy with prospects."

She slipped her arm through his. "I already know you're a nice guy. If you weren't, I wouldn't be here."

He escorted her out of the station by a back way, and opened the door of his fancy sports car for her. "I know of a great seafood place," he said. "Does that sound good?"

Thanks to the strange case of flu that had over-taken her in recent days, Carly didn't have much of an appetite for anything. But she smiled and tried to look enthusiastic as she nodded.

"I've got to ask you a question," she said when they were zipping along the freeway. "How did you know it was over between Mark and me?"

Jim gave her a sidelong look. "He told me. Like I said once, Carly, I've known Mark for a long time."

Carly bit down on her lower lip to keep from asking what Mark had said about her. Probably Jim was one of those buddies he'd talked about, the ones he'd bet that he'd never fall in love.

She didn't care, damn it. She *wouldn't* care.

"If you love Mark," Jim said reluctantly, "don't write him off just yet. Between getting custody of his son and what's happened to Jeanine, I don't guess he's thinking straight. He needs some time to adjust."

"He's planning to 'adjust' in San Francisco—or didn't he tell you that?"

"He told me."

Carly gazed out the window for a long time; there was an emotional storm gathering inside her and she didn't want Jim to see her face. "I love him," she said presently in a small, choked voice, "but it's probably better that we ended it when we did. Mark is temperamental—I would have spent the rest of my life walking on eggshells, worrying that I'd offended him somehow. Who needs it?''

Jim chuckled ruefully. "What am I doing? I should be trying to impress you with what a terrific guy I am." He paused to draw a deep breath, then let it out again. "Carly, Mark isn't a temperamental man—he's practical and pragmatic, like any good journalist. None of this stuff is typical of him."

Carly finally dared to look at Jim again. "What are you saying?"

"That meeting you caused some kind of upheaval in Mark's emotions. If I know him—and believe me, I do—he's still reeling from the shock. Given time and distance, he'll realize he's being a jerk."

Although she had no intention of waiting around for Mark to forgive her, Carly was comforted by Jim's words. They gave her hope that one day the hurting would stop and she could go on with her life without limping inwardly. "I have this friend who wants to go out with you," she said, remembering Janet's request to be "fixed up" with Jim.

He grinned. "The good-looking one with the grocery bag who was standing in the hall the first time we went out?"

Carly nodded, smiling. "That's Janet. She's a wonderful person."

Jim laughed. "We're a pair, you and I. Will somebody tell me why I'm sitting next to one of the most beautiful women in America, extolling the virtues of some other guy?"

"That's easy," Carly answered softly. "It's because you're a sensational person yourself. Watch out, Jim—I'm starting to get the idea that there might be a few nice men out there after all."

Dinner was enjoyable, though Carly wasn't able to eat much. After Jim brought her home, she took a bubble bath and went to bed with a book. And her thoughts strayed to Mark with every other word.

On Friday afternoon, her extra clothes and sleeping bag stuffed into a canvas backpack, Carly got into her car and drove southeast to the town of Bend, where the river expedition would begin. It was late when she finally found the riverside park where the others had camped, and she noticed first thing that the mosquitoes were out in force.

"Don't be a negative thinker," she muttered to herself, getting out her backpack and making her way toward the camp.

The others were gathered around a huge bonfire, and they all looked at home in their skins, as Carly's grandmother used to say. It was evident that river rafting was nothing new to most of them, but Carly already had motion sickness just thinking about it.

Wearing her trusty smile, along with jeans, hiking boots, a flannel shirt and a lightweight jacket, she joined the gathering.

The house Mark selected was in a good part of San Francisco, just far enough from his parents' place to promote good relations. The windows in his den offered a view of the Bay, and Nathan wouldn't have to change schools in the fall.

To Mark's way of thinking, the place was perfect.

Except, of course, for the fact that Carly wasn't there.

He reached into the pocket of his corduroy sports jacket and touched the bracelet she'd dropped through the mail slot at the house in Portland. Sometimes he fancied that he could feel her warmth and incredible energy still vibrating through the metal.

With a sigh, Mark stepped closer to the windows and fixed his gaze on the Bay. The furniture wouldn't arrive for another week, so there was no place to sit.

Life without Carly was like running in a three-legged race, he reflected; what should have given him more mobility and freedom only made it more awkward to move. He thrust his hand through his hair.

"Dad?"

He turned to see Nathan standing uncertainly in the doorway. "Am I allowed in here?" he asked.

Mark frowned. "Why wouldn't you be?"

Nathan lifted one of his small shoulders in a shrug. "Mom didn't like me to go in her living room. She was afraid I'd spill something on the carpet."

With some effort, Mark kept himself from expressing his irritation. Being annoyed with Jeanine wouldn't do anyone any good. "Things are different here, big guy," he said as the boy came to stand beside him. "We're not going to worry much about the carpets."

Nathan looked up at him and flashed the gapped grin that always gave Mark's heart a little twist. "I used to have to go to bed at nine o'clock," he said, obviously hoping Mark would shoot another rule down in flames.

"You still do," Mark replied.

"Darn."

"Hello!" a feminine voice called suddenly in the distance. "Is anybody home?"

"Grandma," Mark and Nathan told each other in chorus, and left the room to go down the stairs and greet Helen.

"I've come bearing gifts," she said, indicating the striped bucket of take-out chicken she carried in one arm. "Am I invited to stay for dinner?"

Mark smiled at his mother, while Nathan rushed forward to collect the chicken.

"She can stay, can't she?" the boy asked, looking back over his shoulder.

"No," Mark teased. "We're going to hold her up for the chicken and then shove her out through the mail slot."

The three of them ate in the spacious, brightly lit kitchen, at a card table borrowed from the elder Holbrooks. When the meal was over, Mark sent Nathan upstairs to take his bath.

"I still think both of you should be staying at our house," Helen fretted when she and Mark were alone.

Mark grinned and shook his head. "We're having a great time camping out in sleeping bags and living on fast food."

"If you're having such a 'great time,'" Helen ventured shrewdly, "then how do you account for that heartache I see in your eyes?"

Mark's grin faded. "It shows, huh?"

Helen nodded. "Yes. Mark, when are you going to admit you were wrong, fly up to Portland and ask that lovely young lady to forgive you?"

He sighed, glad his mother couldn't possibly know how many times he'd made plans to do just that, only to stop himself at the last second. Carly was just getting started on her career, and he had to make a solid home for Nathan. He told himself it would be better if they just went their separate ways.

"She's already dating Jim Benson," he said, hoping that would throw Helen off the subject for good. "I was a passing fancy."

"Nonsense. When the two of you were in a room together, the air crackled. I don't care if she's dating Bruce Willis and Tom Cruise on alternate nights—Carly loves *you.*"

Mark was fresh out of patience. "Well, I don't love her—okay?"

"Liar," Helen responded implacably. "Don't you think I can see what's happening to you? You're being eaten alive by the need to see her."

"You've been reading too many romance novels, Mother," Mark replied evenly. What she said was true, he reflected to himself, and he damned her for knowing it.

Helen got out of her chair with a long-suffering sigh and began gathering up the debris from their impromptu dinner, only to have Mark stop her and take over the task himself. He wasn't about to start depending on other people, even for little things.

When she was gone and Nathan was asleep in a down-filled bag on the floor of his bedroom upstairs, Mark got out his portable computer, set it on the card table and switched it on. After a few minutes of thought, he slipped in a fresh disc and poised his fingers over the keyboard.

"Carly," he typed without consciously planning to.

"Now that's brilliant, Holbrook," he said to himself. "Neil Simon is probably sweating blood."

He sat back in his chair, cupping his hands behind his head, and closed his eyes. In his mind he saw Carly dancing with Jim Benson that night when she'd insisted on keeping her date with the guy. And even though Benson was one of the best friends he'd ever had, his nerve endings jangled just to think of another man holding Carly, kissing her, taking her to bed.

He cursed. Carly wasn't going to go to bed with Jim or anyone else, not for a while, he told himself. She was too sensible for that.

Then he recalled the way she'd responded to him, the soft, greedy sounds she'd made as he pleasured her, the way she'd moved beneath him. His loins tightened painfully, and her name rose to his throat in an aching mass. She was a healthy, passionate woman and, in time, she would want the release a man's body could give her.

In anguish, Mark thrust himself out of his chair and stormed across the room to the telephone. He picked it up from the floor and punched out her number before he could stop himself, not knowing what he would say, needing to hear the sound of her voice.

Her machine picked up, and Mark leaned against the wall in mingled disappointment and relief. "Hi, this is Carly," the recorded announcement ran. "If you're a friend, I'm off braving the wilds of the Deschutes River, and I'll be back on Tuesday morning. If you're a potential burglar, I'm busy bathing my Doberman pinscher, Otto. Either way, leave a message after the beep. Bye."

Mark closed his eyes and swallowed, unable to speak even if he'd had words to say. He hadn't expected hearing her voice to hurt so much, or to flood his mind and spirit with so many memories.

He replaced the receiver gently and went back to his computer, but no words would come to him. Finally he turned the machine off and went upstairs, where he looked in on Nathan.

The boy was sleeping soundly, a stuffed Ewok he wouldn't have admitted to owning within easy reach. Mark smiled sadly, closed the door and went on to his own room.

It was more of a suite, actually, with its own sizable bathroom and a sitting area that had probably been a nursery at one time. The walls were papered in pink-and-white stripes, the floor was carpeted in pale rose, and the place had an air about it that brought whimsical things to mind—sugar and spice and everything nice.

He allowed himself another bleak smile, imagining a baby girl with Carly's big blue-green eyes and tousled blond hair. The knowledge that such a child might never exist practically tore him apart.

Resolutely Mark stepped out of the sitting room and closed the door behind him. In the morning, he told himself, he'd see about having it redone to suit a confirmed bachelor.

Carly unrolled her sleeping bag and spread it out on the ground near two other women who hadn't bothered to include her in their conversation. The photographer the newspaper had sent along was a man—a very uncommunicative man.

After removing her boots, she crawled into the bag in her jeans and shirt, listening to the hooting of an owl and the quiet, whispering rush of the river.

The sky was bejeweled with stars, and the tops of ponderosa pines swayed in the darkness. It was all poetically beautiful, and there was a rock poking against Carly's left buttock.

She got out of the bag with a sigh and moved it over slightly, but when she lay down again, the ground was still as hard and ungiving as ever. A desolate feeling overcame her; she was surrounded by strangers, and Mark didn't love her anymore.

She began to cry, her body shaking with sobs she silenced by pressing the top of the sleeping bag against her mouth. It wasn't fair. Nothing in the whole damn world was fair.

After a long time Carly fell into a fitful, exhausted sleep, and she awakened with a start, what seemed like only minutes later, to find the gung-ho leader crouching beside her.

He was handsome, if you liked the Rambo type, but Carly wasn't charmed by his indulgent grin or his words. "Wake up, Girl Scout," he said. "Everybody else is practically ready to jump into the rafts."

Horrified, Carly bolted upright, squirmed out of the sleeping bag and was instantly awash in nausea. She ran for the log shower rooms.

When she came out feeling pale and shaky and having done what absolutions she could manage, an attractive dark-haired woman wearing khaki shorts and a plaid cotton blouse was waiting. There was a camera looped around her neck.

"Feeling better?" she asked, offering a smile and a handshake. "My name is Hope McCleary, and I didn't come on this trip willingly."

Carly swallowed, glad to see a friendly face. "Carly Barnett," she answered. "And I was sort of shanghaied myself—I'm doing a piece for a newspaper."

Hope grinned. "With me it's a magazine. I work for a regional publication in California."

Carly felt a little better now that she'd found a buddy.

The two women walked back to the campsite together, and Hope helped Carly roll up her sleeping bag and stow it, with her backpack, in one of the rafts. The stuff was carefully covered with a rubber tarp.

Rambo sauntered over and looked Carly up and down with disapproving eyes. "You missed breakfast," he said.

Carly felt her stomach quiver.

"Maybe she wasn't hungry, all right?" Hope snapped, putting her hands on her hips and glaring at him. "Give her a break!"

Rambo backed off, and Carly looked at Hope with undisguised admiration. "Admit it—you're really an angel sent to convince me that life is worth living after all.''

Hope grinned and shook her head. ''I'm no angel, honey, but you're right about part of it—life is *definitely* worth living.'' She paused to pull in a breath. ''Like I said, I'm just a humble magazine editor from San Francisco. Where do you live, Carly, and what newspaper do you write for?''

A pang went through Carly at the mention of the city that had charmed her so much. She might have visited it often if things had worked out between her and Mark. ''I'm from Portland—my managing editor wants the scoop on adventure among executives. I guess I'm lucky he didn't want me to run with the bulls in Palermo.''

Hope laughed and laid a hand on Carly's shoulder. ''A woman called Intrepid,'' she said. ''But you are a little green around the gills. Are you sure you wouldn't prefer to stay here and just question everybody when we get back?''

Carly would have given her rhinestone tiara for a room at the Best Western down the highway, but she wasn't about to let the weak side of her nature win out. ''I'm going on this trip,'' she said firmly.

Soon they were seated in one of the rafts, wearing damp, musty-smelling orange life preservers and listening to Rambo's final speech of the morning. Everybody, he said, was responsible for doing their share of paddling. His eyes strayed to Carly when he added that one slacker could send a raft spinning into the rocks.

She sat determinedly on the wet bench, her jeans already soaked with river water, staring Rambo in the eye and silently praying that she wouldn't throw up.

Soon they were off, skimming down the river between mountains fringed with ponderosas and jack pines. The dirt on the banks had a red cast to it, and here and there the color had seeped into the trunks of trees. Carly got over being scared and was soon paddling for all she was worth.

Diamond-clear water sprayed her, and her morning coffee rose to her throat a couple of times, but all in all the experience was exhilarating.

The convoy of three large rafts traveled until noon, then Rambo led them ashore for lunch. Shivering with cold and with the delight of finding a new area where she was competent, Carly drank coffee and cheerfully chatted with the others.

After thirty minutes Rambo herded them all back into the boats again and they were off.

Several breathless hours later they stopped for the night, making camp in a glade where a stone circle marked the site of the last bonfire.

Carly plundered through her backpack for dry clothes, then went into the woods to change. When she returned, there was a fire blazing and food was being brought out of the boats in large, lightweight coolers.

Reminding herself that a Girl Scout always plans ahead, Carly hung her wet jeans and shirt on a bush, with the underwear secreted behind them.

She jumped when she turned and came face-to-face with Rambo. He was grinning down at her as though she'd just greased herself with chicken fat and entered a body-building competition.

"What was your name again?" he asked. Apparently, now that he'd decided Carly had a right to live, he was going to be chummy.

She barely stopped herself from answering, *Call me Intrepid.* "It's Carly," she said aloud. "Carly Barnett. And you're...?"

His dark brows drew together in a frown. "Weren't you listening during orientation?" he demanded. "It's John. John Walters. Remember that." Displeased again, he turned and stormed away.

Carly raised one hand to her forehead in a crisp salute.

Hope came to her, laughing. "Come on, Carly— let's go gather some wood before he decides you're plotting a mutiny."

"I just can't seem to please that guy," Carly told her friend, following Hope into the woods.

"Do you want to?" Hope asked over one shoulder.

Carly chuckled. She was feeling stronger by the minute. It was nice to know she was a survivor, that she wasn't going to die just because Mark had left her without so much as a backward look. "No, actually. There's bad karma between Rambo and me."

They found enough dry wood to fill their arms and returned to camp.

"Have you ever thought about writing for a magazine?" Hope asked as they dropped the firewood beside the blaze in the middle of the clearing.

Carly shrugged. "No, but that doesn't mean I wouldn't like to try it. Why?"

"You're obviously a very special lady, Carly, and I'm looking for someone to replace a staff writer at the end of the month. Could you send me some clips as soon you get back to Portland?"

Carly was intrigued. Mentally she sorted through the pieces she'd done for the *Times*—the inside view of the shelter for battered women, the rebuttal to Mark's article on fathers' rights, the coverage of the food contest. "I don't have much, I'm afraid," she said finally. "I haven't been working for the paper all that long."

Hope shrugged. "Just send me what you can," she said.

That night was pleasant in a bittersweet sort of way. Everyone sat around the camp fire, full of roasted hot dogs, light beer and potato salad, and sang to the accompaniment of John Walters's guitar. The pungent perfume of the pines filled the air, and the river sang a mystical song begun when the Ice Age ended.

And Carly's heart ached fit to break because Mark wasn't there beside her calling her Scoop. She wondered now why she'd been so insulted at his jibes over her title; it seemed clear, in retrospect, that he'd only been teasing.

"Who was he?" Hope asked as they rolled their sleeping bags out, side by side, within six feet of the fire. Some of the other people had small tents, but most were stretching out under the stars.

"Who?" Carly countered, hedging. She didn't know whether talking about Mark would ease her heartache or get her started on another crying jag.

"The guy who left you with that puppy-loose-on-a-freeway look in your eyes, that's who."

Carly sat down and squirmed into her bag. "Just somebody I used to work with," she said. *And sleep with,* added a voice in her mind. *And love.*

Hope was looking up at the splendor of the night sky, her hands cupped behind her head. Her voice was too low to carry any farther than Carly's ears. "You're going to have his baby, aren't you?"

For a moment the ground seemed to rock beneath Carly's sleeping bag. Her hands moved frantically to her flat abdomen, and her mind raced through the pages of a mental calendar.

"Oh, my God," she whispered, squeezing her eyes shut.

"Sorry," Hope said sincerely. "I thought you'd already figured it out."

Carly sank her teeth into her lower lip. The nausea, the volatile emotions—she should have known.

"What are you going to do?" Hope asked.

"I have no idea," Carly managed to say. But there were things she did know. She was going to have the baby, and she was going to raise it herself. Beyond that, she couldn't think.

"You should tell him, whoever he is," Hope said.

"Yeah," Carly agreed halfheartedly. Mark had a right to know he was going to have another child, but she wasn't sure she had the courage to tell him. He might think she was trying to rope him into a relationship he didn't want, or he could hire lawyers and take the child away from her. After all, he'd planned to sue Jeanine for custody of Nathan.

Hope was quiet after that, and Carly lay huddled in her sleeping bag, imagining the ordeals of labor and birth with no one to lend moral support. After a long time she fell asleep.

She woke with the birds, went off to the woods to be sick and began another day.

That morning her raft overturned, and she and Hope and eight other people were dumped into the icy river. As Carly fought the current, her mouth and nose filled with water, her eyes blinded by the spray, she prayed. *Please God, don't let anything happen to my baby.*

She made it to shore, half-drowned and gasping for breath, and so did everyone else who'd been spilled out of the raft, but their sleeping bags and backpacks were gone.

A comradery had formed between the travelers, though, and the others pooled their extra clothes to help those who'd lost their packs. Rambo had spare blankets in the lead raft.

"This is going to make one hell of a story," Hope said as she stood on the shore beside Carly, soaking wet, snapping pictures as the overturned raft was hauled toward the bank.

Carly could only nod. When she got back to the office, she was going to ask Mr. Clark for a nice, easy assignment—something like skydiving, or jumping over nineteen cars on a motorcycle.

For all of it, she was sorry the next afternoon when the trip ended and pickup trucks hauled the exhausted, exhilarated rafters back to the original camp.

Since Carly had lost everything but the clothes she'd been wearing when the raft tipped over the day before, she was spared the task of packing her gear. She and Hope stood by her car, talking.

"Be sure you send me those clippings, now," Hope said as the two women hugged in farewell.

Carly smiled and nodded. She was never going to forget what a good friend Hope had been to her on this crazy trip. "Take care," she said, slipping behind the wheel of her car.

That day's spate of morning sickness had already passed, and Carly was possessed of a craving for something sweet. She stopped at a doughnut shop and bought two maple bars that were sagging under the weight of their frosting.

"Here's to surviving," she said, taking a bite.

The drive back to Portland was long and uneventful. When Carly arrived, she staggered into the bathroom, without bothering to look through her mail or play her telephone messages, and took a long, steaming-hot shower.

When she'd washed away the lingering chill of the river and the aches and pains inherent in sleeping on the ground, she ate another maple bar, brushed her teeth and collapsed into bed.

Arriving at the paper the next morning, she immediately shut herself up with her computer and started outlining her article. She barely raised her eyes when Mike Fisher, the photographer who'd been sent on the trip with her but kept mostly to himself, brought in black-and-white prints.

Carly flipped through them, smiling. Her favorite showed her crawling out of the river with her hair hanging in her face in dripping tendrils and every line in her body straining for breath. *And for her talent, ladies and gentlemen,* she thought whimsically, *Miss United States will nearly drown.*

She made a mental note to ask for a copy of the photograph, then went back to work. Almost as an afterthought, she asked Emmeline to clip her articles from back issues and send them to Hope in San Francisco.

A full week went by before Carly allowed herself to dream of moving to California and joining the staff of one of the most successful magazines published on the West Coast. When Hope called and offered her a job at an impressive salary, Carly accepted without hesitation.

Maybe she couldn't have Mark Holbrook, but nobody was going to take San Francisco away from her.

10

Janet gave Carly a tearful hug in the parking lot behind their building. "Be happy, okay?" she said.

Carly nodded. Happiness was a knack she hadn't quite mastered yet, but she had the baby to look forward to and the challenge of another new job in another new city. "You, too," she replied. Janet was dating Jim Benson regularly, and things looked promising for them.

The two women parted, and Carly got behind the wheel of her car and began the drive to San Francisco. She would live in a hotel until she found an apartment, and her dad was breaking all precedent to fly out for a short visit.

Carly wanted to tell him about the baby in person.

As she wended her way out of Portland, she considered his possible reactions. After all, in Don Barnett's day women just didn't have babies and raise them alone—they married the father, preferably before but sometimes after conception.

Mentally Carly began to rehearse what she would say. By the time she drove into San Francisco two days later, she had her story down pat.

When Carly checked in at the St. Dominique Hotel, she was told that her father had arrived and wanted her to call his room immediately.

He met her in the hotel lobby, looking like a real-estate agent in his black slacks, white shirt and blue polyester sports jacket. His graying brown hair was still thick, and his skin was tanned. Carly was pleased to realize he'd been spending a reasonable amount of time out of doors, away from the filling station.

She hugged him. "Hi, Dad."

Don kissed her lightly on the forehead. "Hello, doll," he answered, and his voice was gruff with emotion.

Carly was tired from her trip, and she wanted to have something light to eat and lie down for a while, but she knew her dad had been eagerly awaiting her arrival. She couldn't let him down. "How was the flight out?" she asked as she dropped her room key into her purse.

He grinned broadly. "Wasn't bad at all. In fact, there was this cute little stewardess passing out juice—"

Carly laughed. "They call them 'flight attendants' now, Dad. But I can see that you're up-to-date on your flirting."

He smiled at that, but there was a look in his eyes that Carly found disturbing. "For all this success you're having," he said as they gravitated toward one of the hotel's restaurants, "there's something really wrong. What is it, button?"

Tears were never very far from the surface during these hectic days, and Carly had to blink them back. She waited until they'd been seated in a quiet corner of the restaurant before answering. "Dad, I hate to be so blunt, but it wouldn't be fair to beat around the bush. I'm pregnant, and there's no prospect of a wedding."

Don was quiet for a long moment, his expression unreadable. But then he reached out and closed a strong, work-callused hand over Carly's. "That character with the Pulitzer prize?" he asked.

"I knew I should have blacked his eyes."

Carly couldn't help smiling at her dad's phrasing. "That's him," she said. Her eyes filled, and this time there was nothing she could do about it.

"Does he know?"

"Not yet. I'll send him a registered letter after I'm settled."

Her father looked nonplussed. "That's what I like to see—the warm, human touch."

Carly averted her eyes. "It's the best I can do for now. I'm taking things one minute at a time."

"You in love with him?"

Carly sighed. "Yeah," she admitted after a long moment. "But I'll make it through this, Dad." She paused, thinking of that black-and-white photograph of her crawling out of the Deschutes River. "I'm a survivor."

"There's more to life than just surviving, Carly. You shouldn't be hurting like this—you deserve the best of everything."

"You're prejudiced," Carly informed him as a waiter brought menus and water.

Don studied his choices and chose a clubhouse sandwich while Carly selected a salad. During the meal they discussed the latest gossip in Ryerton and Carly's prospects of finding an apartment at a rent she could afford.

"You need money?" her dad asked when they'd finished eating and were riding up in the elevator.

Carly shook her head. "There's still some from the endorsements I did," she answered.

"But a baby costs a lot," Don argued.

She waggled a finger at him. "I'll handle it, Dad," she said.

At the door of her room, he kissed her forehead. "You go on in and take a nap," he ordered. "As for me, I'm headed over to take the tour at the chocolate factory.''

Carly touched his face. ''We have a date for dinner, handsome—don't you dare stand me up.''

''Wouldn't think of it,'' he answered. ''It isn't every day a fella gets to go out on the town with a former Miss United States on his arm.''

With a laugh and a shake of her head, Carly ducked inside her room and closed the door.

There were a dozen yellow rosebuds waiting in a vase on the desk. The card read, *Welcome aboard, Carly. I'm looking forward to working with you. Hope.*

Carly drew in the luscious scent of the roses and made a mental note to call Hope and thank her as soon as she'd had a shower and a brief nap. When she awakened, though, it was late, and she had to rush to dress and get her makeup done.

Wearing a pink-and-white floral skirt and blouse, Carly met her father in the lobby, bringing along one of the rosebuds for his lapel. They had dinner at a place on the Wharf, then took in a new adventure movie.

The next morning Carly called Hope first thing, thanked her for the flowers and made arrangements to meet for lunch. Hope said she'd had her assistant working on finding an apartment for

Carly, and there were several good prospects for her to look at.

"You're spoiling me," Carly protested.

"Nothing is too good for you, kid. Besides, I want to hook you before you find out what a slave driver I am."

Carly laughed, and the two women rang off. Three hours later they met at one of the thousand-and-one fish places on the Wharf for lunch.

"I can see where Carly gets her good looks," Hope said to Don when the two had been introduced.

Don blushed with pleasure, and Carly reminded herself that he was still a young man. Half the single women in Ryerton were probably chasing him.

Lunch was pleasant, but it ended quickly, since Hope had a busy schedule back at the magazine's offices. Carly promised to report for duty at nine sharp the following Monday, then accepted the list of apartments Hope's assistant had checked out for her.

She and her father spent the afternoon taxiing from one place to another, and the last address on the list met Carly's requirements. It was a large studio with a partial view of the water, and it cost more to lease for six months than her dad had paid to buy his first house outright.

Carly left a deposit with the resident manager, then she and Don went back to the hotel.

She was exhausted, and after calling the moving company in Portland to give them her new address, she ordered a room-service dinner for herself and Don. They had a good time together seated at the standard round table beside the window, watching a pay-movie on TV while they ate.

"You going to be okay if I go back home tomorrow?" Don asked when the movie was over and room service had collected the debris from their meal. "I hate to leave you way out here all by yourself. It's not like you couldn't find somebody in Ryerton who'd be proud to be your husband—"

Carly laid her index finger to his lips. "Not another word, Gramps. San Francisco is my town—I know it in my bones—and I'm going to stay here and make a life for myself and my baby."

Respect glimmered in her father's ice-blue eyes. "Maybe you could come home for Christmas," he said.

"Maybe," Carly answered, her throat thick.

Her dad left then, and Carly took a brief bath, then crawled into bed and fell asleep. She didn't open her eyes again until the reception desk gave her a wake-up call.

Carly and Don had breakfast together, then he kissed her goodbye and set out for the airport in a cab. Even though he'd obviously been reluctant to leave her, he'd been eager, too. The filling station was the center of his life, and he wanted to get back to it.

At loose ends, Carly went to the offices of *Californian Viewpoint* to tell Hope she'd found an apartment.

Hope was obviously rushed, but she took the time to show Carly the office assigned to her.

"You didn't forget," Carly began worriedly, "that I'm pregnant?"

Hope shook her head, and her expression was kind and watchful. "I didn't forget, Barnett. And your dad told me who the father is—I must say, I'm impressed. With genes like yours and Holbrook's, that kid of yours is going to have it all."

Carly laid her hands to her stomach and swallowed. "I should skin Dad for spilling the beans like that. When, pray tell, did he manage to work *that* little tidbit into the conversation?"

Hope smiled. "When we were having lunch and you went to the rest room. Does Mark know you're here in San Francisco, Carly?"

"No," Carly said quickly. Guiltily. "And he doesn't know I'm pregnant yet, either, so if this is one of those small-world things and he's a friend of yours, kindly don't tell him."

Cocking her head to one side and folding her arms, Hope replied, "It is a small world, Carly. I went to college with Mark."

Carly sighed. "I suppose that means I'm going to be running into him a lot," she said.

Hope was on her way to the door. "Worse," she said, tossing the word back over one shoulder. "I want you to interview him about his new play." With that, Carly's new boss disappeared, giving her employee no chance to protest.

There was no escape, and Carly knew it. She'd signed a lease on an expensive apartment and she needed her job. She was going to have to face Mark Holbrook, in person, and tell him she was carrying his child.

All through the weekend she practiced what she would say and how she'd say it. She'd be cool, dignified, poised. Mark could have visitation rights if he wanted them, she would tell him. If he offered to pay child support, she would thank him politely and accept.

Despite two solid days of rehearsal, though, Carly was not prepared when she rang the doorbell at Mark's town house at ten-thirty Monday morning.

Nathan answered, and his freckled face lit up when he saw who'd come to call. "Carly!" he cried.

She smiled at him, near tears again. "Yeah," she answered. "Learn any good card tricks lately?"

The child nodded importantly and stepped back to admit her. "You're here to see my dad, aren't you?" he asked, his voice and expression hopeful. "He's really going to be surprised—he was expecting a reporter."

He's going to be more surprised than you'd ever guess, Carly thought, but she smiled at Nathan and nodded. "Where is he?"

"I'll get him," Nathan offered eagerly.

Carly shook her head. "I'd rather not be announced, if that's okay with you."

The boy looked puzzled. "All right. Dad's in his office—it's up those stairs."

Carly drew a deep breath, muttered a prayer and marched up the stairway and along the hall.

Mark was sitting at his computer, his back to her, his hands cupped behind his head.

Carly felt a pang that nearly stopped her heartbeat. "Hello, Mark," she said when she could trust herself to talk.

He swiveled in his chair and then launched himself from it, his face a study in surprise.

All weekend Carly had been hoping that when she actually saw Mark, she'd find herself unmoved. The reality was quite the opposite; if anything, she loved him more than she had before.

His expressive brown eyes moved over her, pausing ever so briefly, it seemed to Carly, at her expanding waistline. "What are you doing here?" he asked, his tone lacking both unkindness and warmth.

Carly shrugged. "I'm supposed to interview you for *Californian Viewpoint.*"

"What?"

"I work there," she explained, wondering how she could speak so airily when her knees were about to give out.

"You've living in San Francisco?"

She nodded.

"Oh." Mark looked distracted for a moment, then said abruptly, "Sit down. Please."

Gratefully Carly took a seat in a comfortable leather chair. Her hands trembled as she pulled her notebook out of her oversize handbag, along with a pencil. "Hope tells me you're writing a new play."

Mark looked confused. "Hope?"

"McCleary. Editor of *Californian Viewpoint* and your friend from college."

"Oh, yeah," Mark replied, and his gaze dropped to Carly's stomach again. Was the man psychic?

Carly crossed her legs at the knee and smoothed her soft cotton skirt. "A photographer will be along in a few minutes," she said. "Before we get started, how's Jeanine doing?"

Although Mark still looked a little off balance, he was obviously recovering. The ghost of a grin tugged at one corner of his mouth. "She's out of the hospital and attending regular AA meetings," he answered.

"Obviously Nathan is still with you."

Mark nodded. "He's had a lot of upheaval in his life during the past few years. Jeanine and I agreed not to jerk him back and forth between her place and mine."

In the distance the doorbell chimed, and Mark frowned at the sound.

"My photographer," Carly said brightly, though she begrudged the precious few moments she'd had with Mark and didn't want to share him.

"Great," Mark said, and the word was raspy.

Carly had been introduced to Allen Wright, the photographer, that morning in Hope's office. Besides his talent with a camera, she'd learned, he was a computer whiz.

True to form, Allen barely greeted Carly and Mark before zeroing in on Mark's computer and looking it over. A handsome young man with brown hair and blue eyes, he turned to grin at the master of the house. "Nice piece of equipment," he remarked.

Mark was looking at Carly; she could feel the heat and weight of his eyes. That extraordinary brain of his was probably developing one-second X rays of her uterus. "Yeah," he said pensively. "Great equipment."

Carly urged Allen to take the candidly posed photos needed for the layout and then shuffled him out the door.

When he was gone, she turned to Mark, her eyes feeling big, her teeth sunk into her lower lip. She was going to have to tell him now but, God help her, she couldn't find the words.

He made it all unnecessary. "My baby?" he asked in a husky voice, his gaze dropping again to Carly's stomach.

Her face flushed with color. "Who told you?" she demanded. "My Dad? Hope?"

"Nobody had to tell me," Mark said, shoving splayed fingers through his hair.

Carly picked up her notebook again. "Let's just get the interview out of the way, okay? Then we can go our separate ways."

Mark shocked her by wrenching the notebook from her hand and flinging it across the room. "How the hell can you be so calm about this?" he demanded. He was gripping her upper arms now, forcing her to look at him. "Did you think I was just going to say, 'Oh, that's nice,' and read off my entry in *Who's Who* for your damned article?"

Carly pulled free. "I told you about the baby, Mark. That's the end of my obligation."

"The hell it is," he grated.

Carly's old fear that Mark might want to take her child from her when it was born resurfaced in a painful surge. "I'd better send someone else to do the interview," she said stiffly.

With a harsh sigh, he turned away from her. "I'd rather just get it over with, if it's all the same to you."

Legs trembling, Carly made her way back to her chair and sank gratefully into it. Mark picked up her notebook and brought it back to her.

"I want a place in this baby's life, Carly," he said.

She nodded briskly, unable to look at his face, composed herself and asked, "How's the new play going?"

"Well enough," Mark answered, falling into his own chair. "But I think I prefer nonfiction."

It was a relief to have things on a professional level again. "Does that mean you'll be going back into the newspaper business?"

He considered the question for a long moment, then shook his head. "I think I'd like to do books," he responded finally.

"Starting with?"

"One about what's happening in China, I think. There's more than one kind of revolution going on there, obviously. I'd like to write about how the cultural and political conflicts interweave."

"Doesn't the prospect of danger bother you?" Carly asked, only marginally aware that *she* was the one troubled by the idea of Mark risking life and limb.

He lifted one shoulder in a shrug. "There are a lot of hazards in everyday life," he reasoned. "I can't hide in a closet, hoping the sky won't fall on my head."

Carly lowered her eyes for a moment, then shifted the conversation back to the craft of writing plays. "How about your *Broken Vows?*" she asked moderately. "Whatever became of that?"

Mark smiled sadly. "Not a subtle question, Scoop, but I'll answer it anyway. Edina sold it to a movie producer, and it's being filmed in Mendocino even as we speak."

Shock and fury flowed through Carly's veins like venom, and she scooted forward in her chair. "After all you put me through, Mark Holbrook, you went ahead and *sold* that play?"

He nodded. "I read it and decided I'd been a jerk about the whole thing."

Carly recalled Jim Benson saying that Mark would eventually come to exactly that realization.

It was too bad, she reflected to herself, that he hadn't felt any compunction to tell *her* about his change of heart.

She supposed there was someone else in his life now, and the thought filled her with pain.

"Well," she said, standing. "I'd better get back to the magazine and start writing." She offered her hand. "Thanks for the interview."

The moment Carly was gone, Mark raced up the stairs, down the hallway and into his bedroom suite. In the nursery a painter's helper was just getting ready to strip the pink-and-white striped paper from the walls.

"Stop!" Mark yelled, making the guy jump in surprise.

He didn't stay to explain, however. He ran back downstairs to his office and flipped through the phone book until he found the number for *Californian Viewpoint.*

When the receptionist answered, he identified himself and asked for Hope.

Carly sat at the computer in her office, her fingers making the keys click with a steady rhythm as she worked on the draft of her article about Mark. A rap at her door interrupted her concentration, and she raised her eyes to see Hope standing in the chasm.

She pulled off her glasses and set them aside on the desk. "I told him," she said.

Hope nodded, her eyes eager. "And what did he say?"

"Not much, actually. He wants to be part of the baby's life."

Hope closed the door. "Didn't he—well—ask you to dinner or anything?"

Carly gave her boss a wry look. "No, Yenta, he didn't," she answered. And then she sighed and sat back in her chair. "This is going to be an odd situation, I can see that right now. It'll be like being divorced from a man I was never married to in the first place."

"There isn't any hope that the two of you might get back together?" The editor looked disappointed, like a kid who'd expected a pony for Christmas and gotten a stick horse instead.

"Even if Mark Holbrook came to me on bended knee," Carly said with lofty resolution, "I wouldn't take him back. He was absolutely impossible when I showed that agent his play—there was no reasoning with him. If you think I want a whole lifetime of *that,* you're a candidate for group therapy."

Hope had drawn up a chair, and she leaned forward in it, looking at Carly in amazement. "You gave someone his play, without even *asking* him about it?"

Carly swallowed. "I know it sounds bad, but you have to consider my motives—"

"What would *you* do if you'd written a play and somebody snitched it and passed it on to an agent?"

"I'd have a fit," Carly answered defensively. "But I'd also forgive that person, especially if I happened to love him."

Hope let out a sigh that made her dark brown bangs rise from her forehead. By tacit agreement the two women dropped the subject of love. "How did the interview go?"

"It was great," Carly answered, her gaze drifting toward the window. She could see a bright red trolley car speeding down a hill, looking for all the world as though it would plunge into the Bay. She swallowed hard. "After all of it, he's letting them produce the play. It's being made into a movie in Mendocino."

"So in a way you won," Hope reasoned, spreading her hands.

"Right," Carly answered forlornly. "I won."

At the end of the day Carly went home to her apartment, where she'd been roughing it, waiting for her furniture to arrive. Her new kitten, Zizi, greeted her at the door with a mewling squeak.

Whisking the little bundle of white fur to her face, Carly nuzzled the cat and laughed. There was something about a baby—no matter what species it was—that always lifted her spirits.

She fed Zizi the nutritious dry food the pet store had recommended, then changed her cotton skirt and blouse for cut-off jeans and tank top. She was just opening a can of diet cola when the telephone rang.

He won't call, Carly lectured herself as she struggled not to lunge for the phone. *So don't get your hopes up.*

For all her preparations, her voice was eager when she lifted the receiver and said, "Hello?"

"Hi, Carly," Janet greeted her. "I'm calling with big news."

Carly closed her eyes for a moment, knowing perfectly well what her friend's announcement would be. She was happy for Janet, of course, but she felt a little left out, too.

"Jim and I are getting married!" Janet bubbled.

Carly smiled. "That's great," she said, and she meant it.

"I want you to be my maid of honor, of course."

Always a bridesmaid, Carly thought. She knew she was feeling sorry for herself, but she couldn't seem to help it. She generated enthusiasm befitting the situation. "What colors are you going to use?"

"Pink and burgundy," Janet answered without hesitation.

Carly remembered when she'd first arrived in Portland, and Janet had been talking about getting married. At that time her ideas about the institution had been practical, but hardly romantic. "Have you decided that love isn't a myth after all?" she asked.

Janet laughed. "Have I ever. Jim's my man and I'm nuts about him." She paused. "Speaking of nuts, have you and Mark been able to touch base or anything?"

Carly sighed. "I interviewed him this morning," she said sadly. "And I told him about the baby."

All the humor was gone from Janet's voice. "Don't tell me he didn't ask you to marry him on the spot?"

"Of course he didn't," Carly replied breezily. "It's over between Mark and me—has been for a long time."

"Right," Janet replied, sounding patently unconvinced. "Now that the two of you are in the same city again, the earthquake people had better keep an eye on the Richter scale."

Carly shook her head. "It's really over, Janet," she insisted. Her words had put a definitive damper on the conversation, and it ended about five minutes later.

Zizi came to amble up Carly's bare legs and sit down on her stomach. "Reooow," she said sympathetically.

"Ain't it the truth?" Carly sighed, sweeping the kitten into one hand as she got back to her feet. She cuddled Zizi for a few moments, then put her down again. There was no sense in moping around the apartment, waiting for a call that was never going to come. She'd go down to the market and pick out some fresh vegetables and fish for supper.

After finding her purse, Carly flipped on her answering machine and left the apartment. She walked to the market, since it was a warm August evening and the sun was still blazing in the sky.

She chose cauliflower, and broccoli and crisp asparagus, then purchased a pound of fresh cod. As she climbed back up the hill to her building, she was filled with a sort of lonely contentment. Maybe her life wasn't perfect—whose was? But she lived in a city she was growing to love, worked at a job that excited her and, come winter, she would be a card-carrying mother.

Those things were enough. They had to be.

Carly didn't know whether to be alarmed or encouraged when she saw Mark's car parked in front of her building. When she went inside, she found him sitting on the bottom step, a big bouquet of pink daisies in his hand.

Her traitorous heart skipped over one beat as he stood, a smile lighting his eyes. He took her grocery bag from her and handed over the flowers.

Carly looked at him with wide, worried eyes. "What do you want?"

"Now there's a cordial greeting," he observed, putting a hand to the small of Carly's back and propelling her gently up the stairs. "I guess I should be grateful you aren't shooting at me from the roof."

"If this is about the baby..." Carly began as she stopped in front of her door and rummaged in her purse for the key.

"It's about you and me," he said in a husky voice. "Carly, I came here to ask you to marry me."

She'd forgotten how old-fashioned Mark could be. Obviously he meant to do his grim duty, however distasteful he might find it.

She stepped into the apartment, snatched her groceries from Mark's arms and shoved the riotously pink daisies at him. "Don't trouble yourself," she snapped, and slammed the door in his face.

11

Carly closed her eyes and leaned against the door, Mark's knock causing the wood to vibrate.

"I'm not leaving until you hear me out, Carly," he called. "And I'm as stubborn as you are—I can keep this up all night, if necessary!"

"Go away!" Carly cried as the kitten, Zizi, brushed her ankles with its fluffy, weightless body.

"I'm not going anywhere," Mark retorted. "Damn it, let me in—I have things to say to you."

Carly shook her head, even though there was no one to see the gesture. "Give me one good reason why I should listen to anything you have to tell me."

He was silent for a moment, and the knocking stopped. "Because inquiring minds want to know," he finally responded.

Carly's lips curved into an involuntary smile. She crossed the room to set her grocery bag and purse on the counter by the stove.

The knocking started again. "Carly!"

She sighed. At this rate the neighbors would be summoning the police any second. "All right, all right," she muttered, returning to the door and sliding the bolt. "Come in!"

Mark stepped inside the spacious studio, looking irritated. He fairly shoved the pink daisies at her. "Here," he snapped.

"Thanks," Carly retorted just as shortly, but there was a softening process going on inside. Mark was getting to her in spite of her efforts to keep him at a distance.

She found a cut-glass vase in one of the cupboards and put the flowers into it with water. Then she set them on the sunny windowsill above the sink.

She stiffened when she felt Mark's hands come to rest, ever so gently, on her shoulders. He said her name hoarsely, and turned her to face him.

"I was wrong."

Carly jutted out her chin. "You can say that again."

The merest hint of a smile flickered in his eyes. "But I won't," he answered. "Carly, I love you. And I need you."

"Why?" she asked in an ironic singsong voice. "You've got everything—a son, money, a career anyone would envy—why do you want me?"

"Why do I want you?" He arched one eyebrow, and his voice was gruff. "Because you gave my life a dimension and a perspective it's never had before or since. With you I was one hundred percent alive, Carly."

She touched her upper lip with the tip of her tongue, watching Mark with wide eyes. "I know what you mean," she admitted softly, reluctantly. "I've got a great job, and I've proven to myself that I can make it on my own. And for all that, something vital is missing."

Mark's dark gaze caressed her. "Please," he said, "give me a chance to prove to you that I'm nothing like that jerk who threw such a fit over a play."

Without moving at all, he had pulled her to him. She came to rest against his strong chest, her body trembling, and he moved his hands over her back, soothing her. She slipped her arms around his waist, telling him physically what she could not say in words.

His lips moved, warm, against her hair. "I know now that I was scared of what I felt for you, Carly—and then there was getting Nathan back and Jeanine's accident. I distanced myself from you, thinking that would keep us both from getting hurt, but it didn't work." He paused to draw in a deep, ragged breath. "I promise I'll never do that again, sweetheart. When we have problems in the future, we'll stand toe-to-toe until they're worked out—agreed?''

Carly lifted her head and nodded. "Agreed."

He curved a finger under her chin. "I love you," he said, and then he lowered his mouth to hers.

Carly gave a little whimper as he kissed her, and her arms went around his neck. The feel of his hard frame against her set her flesh to quivering beneath her clothes.

He rested one of his hands, fingers splayed, against her belly. The muscles there leaped against his palm in response, and Carly smiled as she drew back from the kiss. In a few months he would be able to lay his hand there and feel the movements of their child.

"Marry me," he said, kissing her neck. He unsnapped her jeans and slid his fingers down over the warm flesh of her abdomen to find the swirl of silk.

Carly's head was light, and her eyes weren't focusing properly. She gave a little moan as Mark toyed with her. "Yes," she whispered, "oh, yes..."

He chuckled as he spread his left hand over her bottom, pushing her into the fiery attendance of his right. "It would be convenient if you had a bed, Scoop."

"Oooooh," Carly groaned, closing her eyes and letting her head fall back. During those moments, her every emotion and sense seemed to center on the motion of Mark's fingers.

He left her swaying and dazed in the middle of the room, while he gathered the three large and colorful floor pillows she'd bought in an import shop and arranged them on the floor.

It never occurred to Carly to protest when he came back to her and spread her gently on the pillows, a prize to be examined and savored. He stripped her methodically, kissing her insteps when he'd tossed aside her shoes, nibbling at the undersides of her knees when he'd taken away her cut-off jeans. He removed her T-shirt next, and then, with excruciating slowness, her bra.

Carly cupped her hands beneath her breasts, lifting them to him, offering them. He shed his jacket and shirt and flung them aside before bending, with a low groan of pleasure, to catch one pink gumdrop of a nipple between his teeth.

Carly writhed on the soft pillows, her heels wedged against the hardwood floor, while Mark suckled her. Then he hooked a thumb under the waistband of her panties, her last remaining garment, and drew them down.

She wriggled out of them, kicked them away, and Mark stayed with her breast, as greedy as a thirsty man just then allowed to drink. Desperate, she found his hand and pressed it to the warm, moist delta between her legs.

He chuckled against her nipple and began moving his palm in a slow, titillating circle. Carly's body followed him obediently, yearning for his attentions.

He left her breast to kiss his way down over her belly, and Carly clutched at the floor in anticipation though, of course, the waxed wood would grant her no purchase.

She felt his lips on her still-flat abdomen. "I'm going to make your mom really happy," he promised the little person inside.

A great shudder shook Carly; she knew what Mark was going to do to her, that he would make her perform a physical and spiritual opera before he let her up off those pillows, and she couldn't wait another moment.

"Oh, God, Mark," she whispered, "now—please, now."

He parted her with his fingers, gave her a single flick with his tongue.

Carly cried out in lusty delight, not caring who heard, and sunk her teeth into her lower lip when she felt Mark position himself between her knees. She covered her breasts with her hands, not because she wanted to hide them, but because she could not lie still. Mark made her show herself again.

"I want to see them," he said, his voice low and rumbling. Then he went back to the taut little nubbin of flesh that awaited him so eagerly.

He was greedy, and Carly clamped a hand over her mouth to stifle her cries of pleasure. Immediately, firmly, he removed it, and the gesture told Carly that he would demand an unrestrained response from her. He would hear every sound, see every inch of her flesh.

She gave a series of choked gasps as he took hold of the undersides of her knees, lifting and parting them so she was totally vulnerable to him. And then, having conquered her completely, he was ruthless.

He brought her to a thunderous crescendo that had her writhing beneath his mouth, and the sounds of her triumphant submission echoed off the walls and the ceiling.

She had known he wouldn't permit her to reach only one climax, no matter how soul shattering it might be. His own pleasure was in direct proportion to the heights Carly reached. Still, knowing these things, she pleaded with him.

He only chuckled, nibbling at the inside of her thigh while she came down, trembling and moist with exertion, from the top of a geyser. "We haven't even begun," he said.

Soon she was bobbing on the crest of an invisible spray of energy again, her back arched, her eyes dazed and sightless, her hair clinging to her cheeks and forehead. And Mark was already arousing her anew long before she'd recovered.

The instinct for power gave her the strength to open his jeans and reach inside, pressing her palm against his magnificence, closing her fingers around it.

He groaned, and his wonderful eyes rolled closed. "Oh, Carly..." he grated out. "Carly."

She caressed him until he was muttering in delirium, then maneuvered him so that he was lying sprawled on the pillows, as helpless as Carly had been earlier. She finished stripping him, bold as the queen of some primitive tribe, and bent to touch him lightly with her tongue.

He gave a guttural cry, and Carly felt a sweep of loving triumph. She had Mark where she wanted him, and she wasn't going to let him go until she'd enjoyed him thoroughly, because she had won the battle and he was the spoils.

His submission was glorious, full of honor, and Carly loved him with a sweet and tender violence.

Finally, though, he stopped her, his hands clenched on either side of her head. She watched his powerful chest rise and fall as he struggled for the breath to speak. "Inside you," he managed after a long time. "I want to be inside you."

Carly would not give up her position of dominance—this time it would be Mark who lay beneath the pleasure, drowning in its splendor.

She placed a knee on either side of his hips and guided him to her portal with one hand, smiling when he buckled beneath her in a desperate search.

Splaying her hands over his heaving chest, feeling his nipples tighten under her palms, she allowed him only a little solace. He tossed his head from side to side, half-blinded with the need of her, and Carly loved him all the more for his ability to surrender so completely.

"More?" she teased.

"More," he pleaded.

She was generous, giving him another inch of sanction. His skin was moist beneath her hands, and she could feel an underlying quiver in his muscles as he struggled for control.

He arched his neck, his eyes closed, and Carly bent forward to kiss and nibble the underside of his chin. Then she felt him clasp her hips, and she knew the game was almost over.

Sure enough, he pressed her down onto him in a strong stroke that immediately set her afire. She groaned as he raised his fingers to her nipples and rolled them into tight little buttons.

He made another pass into her, and the tiny muscles where the magic lay went into wild spasms, making Carly toss back her head and cry out over and over again in satisfaction. When she finally went limp, Mark shifted her so that she lay beneath him, and took her in earnest.

At peace, she watched in love and wonder as pleasure moved in his eyes. She spread one hand over his muscular buttocks as he strained to give himself up to her, while the other traced the outline of his lips.

His teeth clamped lightly on her finger when he stiffened suddenly, emptying himself into her. And this time the cry that filled the shadowy room was Mark's, not Carly's.

He fell onto the pillows beside her when it was over, curving an arm around her waist and holding her close against his chest. They lay in silence for a long time, but even then there was some kind of dynamics going on between them.

It was a mystical mating process, fusing their two spirits together at an invisible place. Carly's eyes filled with tears as one indefinable emotion after another swept over her.

She was Mark's, and he was hers, and not just until the next time they disagreed over something, either. By a process she could not begin to understand, an age-old link between them had been reinforced.

Carly kissed Mark's shoulder and closed her eyes.

Beyond the fenced boundaries of the little churchyard, Kansas stretched in every direction. Plump matrons in colorful dresses chattered, while men smoked and talked about their crops and "them politicians back in Washington," whom they held in a healthy and typically American contempt. Children zigzagged throughout, filled with exuberance because the ripe summer was still with them and because there would be cake and punch aplenty at the reception.

Clad in her mother's gossamer wedding dress, her arm linked with Mark's, Carly stood a little closer to her husband. The limo he'd hired to drive them from the church to the reception at the Grange Hall glistened like a sleek silver ghost at the curb.

Carly smiled at the stir it caused.

"Came all the way from Topeka," she heard someone say.

Mark broke off the conversation he'd been having with Carly's father and his own, and grinned down at her. Something unspoken passed between them, and then they were getting into the plush car, Carly grappling with her rustling voluminous skirts of lace and satin. Her bouquet of pink daisies and white rosebuds lay fragrant in her lap.

She gave a happy sigh.

Mark chuckled and leaned over to kiss her cheek. "I love you, Mrs. Holbrook," he said.

She beamed at him, answering with her eyes.

The driver obligingly turned on the stereo, filling the car with soft, romantic music. It was his way of telling the newlyweds, Carly figured, that he wasn't listening in on their conversation.

They talked with their foreheads touching about their brief upcoming honeymoon in Paris. After that, Carly would be returning to San Francisco and Nathan and the magazine, while Mark jetted to the Far East to gather material for his book on China.

Whether or not he would get into the country remained to be seen. Carly suspected he had contacts who would be willing to smuggle him over the border, but she didn't allow herself to think about the possible ramifications of *that*, because she wasn't about to spoil the happiest day of her life.

When the limo pulled up in front of the ramshackle Grange Hall, which had never been painted, there were already a number of wedding guests waiting, and country-and-western music vibrated in the hot August sunshine.

Mark and Carly went inside, and Mark immediately pulled her into his arms for a dance. This delighted the onlookers, who loved a wedding almost as much as a rousing cattle auction.

Playfully Mark touched his lips to hers, and everyone clapped and cheered with delight.

"Show off," Carly said, one hand resting lightly on his nape.

He laughed. "Me? Tell me, Mrs. Holbrook—was *I* the one who put on a quarter of a yard of spandex and twirled flaming batons in front of a whole nation?"

Carly's cheeks warmed. "You're still going to be teasing me about that in fifty years, aren't you?"

Mark pulled her a little closer. "Yup," he said.

After that, Carly danced with her father, then with Mark's father, then with Nathan.

"You look real pretty in that dress," her stepson said.

Carly smiled. "Thanks—you're looking pretty handsome yourself." She wanted to touch his hair, but she held back, unwilling to embarrass him. "You don't mind about my taking your dad away to Paris for a week?" she asked.

Solemnly Nathan shook his head. "And you don't need to worry when he goes to China, either.

I'm pretty tough, and I won't let anybody hurt you."

Carly's heart swelled with love. "Okay," she said. "I won't give it a thought."

Toward the end of the song, Mark tapped his son on the shoulder to cut in. "Judging from the look on your face, I've got some pretty strong competition in that kid."

She smiled, glad to be close to her husband again. "He's one terrific guy," she agreed. "He just told me not to be afraid when you go to China, because he's tough and he can take care of me."

Mark searched her face. "*Are* you worried about me going to China, Scoop?"

"Of course I am," Carly answered. "What kind of wife would I be if I didn't consider the dangers? But I'm determined not to stand in your way where your career is concerned, and I expect the same courtesy from you."

It was time for more photographs and for the cutting of the giant cake decorated with white sugar doves and scallops of pink frosting.

They posed and exchanged sticky, crumbling bites of cake, and a collective sigh of approval arose from the guests when Mark took Carly into his arms and gave her a sound kiss.

"For better or for worse, Mrs. Holbrook," he said, his voice a hoarse whisper, "and for always, I love you."

Happy tears sprang into her eyes for the hundredth time that day. "Could I say something to you?"

He smiled. "Anything, as long as you never say goodbye."

"I'm so glad I met you," Carly told him. "And so glad I'm a survivor."

He kissed her. "So am I, Scoop. So am I."

She gazed up at him with loving eyes. "One more dance before we go?"

Mark nodded.

They whirled around the dance floor, unaware now of the guests, and the teetering cake, and the mountains of beautifully wrapped presents. Mr. and Mrs. Mark Holbrook were, for those precious moments, aware only of each other.

San Francisco One year later...

Carly wore jeans and a blue T-shirt, and the baseball cap Nathan had given her on Mother's Day sat firmly on her head, the brim covering her nape. Riding on her back, papoose style, was Molly, who watched her father approach with solemn aquamarine eyes.

Out on the diamond, Nathan was speeding between third base and home. The ball came in from left field; the pitcher caught it and hurled it to the catcher.

Nathan dived, sliding into home plate on his belly, his hands outstretched.

"Safe!" yelled the umpire, who was, like everybody else on both teams, a kid from the neighborhood.

Reaching the place where his wife and daughter stood, Carly still unaware of his approach, Mark leaned over to give Molly a light kiss on the forehead.

She rewarded him with a gurgling chortle and a, "Da-da!"

Carly spun around at that, her eyes big in her dusty, gamine's face. Her baseball cap fell off onto the ground when she flung her arms around Mark's neck.

He kissed her soundly, even though he knew he'd hear about it from Nathan. In his son's world, a guy just didn't kiss a woman in front of everybody in the neighborhood like that.

"How was China?" Carly asked. Her voice was throaty and low, and her eyes were filled with a blue-green come-hither look.

"Same as always," Mark answered gruffly. He'd made two trips since he and Carly were married. "Big. Isolated. Awesomely beautiful."

"I think we should go home and discuss this," Carly crooned.

He bent to pick up her fallen baseball cap and put it back on her head. This time the brim stuck out to the side, giving her a jaunty, Our Gang kind of look. "You're absolutely right, Mrs. Holbrook," he responded, his body tightening at the luscious prospect of being alone with her in the shadowy privacy of their bedroom. "But what about the short person here?"

Carly grinned. "Molly's due for a nap," she replied, "and Nathan will be out here playing baseball until you come back and drag him home for supper."

He lifted his brown-haired daughter out of the back sling and kissed her glossy curls. "You do look tired, kid," he told the child, his expression serious.

Molly's lower lip curled outward as though he'd insulted her, then she tossed back her head and wailed.

Twenty minutes later, when her mother had washed her face and hands and given her a bottle, Molly closed her enormous Carly eyes and went immediately to sleep.

Mark led his wife out of the nursery and into their bedroom, taking off her baseball cap and tossing it aside. "As for you, Mrs. Holbrook," he said, "you're about to spend some quality time with your husband."

He saw the tremor of pleasure go through her, watched as her cheeks turned a delicious apricot pink. And he knew he loved her as desperately as he ever had.

"Mark," she began shyly, "I need a shower...."

He nodded. "So do I," he answered, catching hold of her T-shirt and lifting it off over her head.

Her breasts, full ever since she'd given birth to Molly, seemed to burgeon over the tops of her lace bra, and the sight of them filled Mark with a grinding ache that would take a long time to satisfy. He anticipated the feeling of a nipple tightening in his mouth, the arch of Carly's body against him, the little purring groans that would escape her throat.

He brought down one side of the bra and bent to taste her.

They undressed each other in a slow, romantic dance they'd learned together, and when they were naked, Carly led Mark into the bathroom. He adjusted the spigots in the double-size shower and drew her underneath the spray of the water with him.

Taking up the soap, Carly turned it beneath her hands, making a lather. Then she began to wash her husband, to prepare him for a sweet sacrifice that would be offered on their bed.

His muscles quivered beneath his flesh as she soaped him all over, gently washing away the loneliness, the grit, the frustration of being parted from her. She was kneeling before him, washing his feet, when she looked up at him through the spray and ran one slippery hand up the inside of his thigh.

He felt his Adam's apple bob in his throat as he swallowed. "Carly," he managed to grind out just as she closed her mouth over him.

He entangled his fingers in her dripping hair and let the crown of his head rest against the shower wall, and he tasted warm water when he opened his mouth to moan in helpless pleasure. She gripped his tensed buttocks then, as though she feared that he would leave her.

His knees weakened as she continued to pleasure him, and he wondered how long he could stand before her. He was on the verge of slipping to the floor of the shower as it was.

"Carly," he choked out, and he tried to lift her head from him, but she would not be deterred.

Only seconds later his raw cry of surrender echoed in the shower stall, stifled by the sound of the water.

* * *

They lay naked in the middle of the bed, arms around each other, legs entwined. Carly's head rested on Mark's shoulder.

"That was your last trip to China," she said, hardly able to believe he'd really said he wouldn't be leaving her again for a long time.

With his hand he cupped her breast possessively. "I'll be underfoot from now on," he said. "Even though I'll be writing a book, your friends will all think I'm a house husband."

Carly laughed, but the sound caught in her throat as Mark's thumb moved back and forth across her nipple. She purred as warm pleasure uncurled within her. "We could use one around here," she said, stretching as Mark continued to stroke her. "You see, the Holbrook family is about to get bigger again."

He reared up on one elbow to search her face with those wonderful, luminous brown eyes of his. "We're having another baby?" he asked hopefully, as though such a thing could happen only once in an aeon.

Carly held up two fingers. "It's a double play, Mr. Holbrook," she answered, her throat thick with emotion, "and our team is about to score."

Mark laughed for joy, and there were tears glistening in his brown eyes, but his body was conducting an independent celebration all its own. He parted Carly's legs and lay between them, letting her feel his heat and his power and his vast love for her.

His face somber again, he slipped his hands under her bottom and lifted, then went into her in one unbroken stroke. And Carly welcomed him with her whole soul.

Mark Holbrook was home to stay.

Take 3 of "The Best of the Best™" Novels FREE
Plus get a FREE surprise gift!

Special Limited-time Offer

Mail to The Best of the Best™

> 3010 Walden Avenue
> P.O. Box 1867
> Buffalo, N.Y. 14269-1867

YES! Please send me 3 free novels and my free surprise gift. Then send me 3 of "The Best of the Best™" novels each month. I'll receive the best books by the world's hottest romance authors. Bill me at the low price of $3.99 each plus 25¢ delivery and applicable sales tax, if any.* That's the complete price and a savings of over 20% off the cover prices—quite a bargain! I understand that accepting the books and gift places me under no obligation ever to buy any books. I can always return a shipment and cancel at any time. Even if I never buy another book from Harlequin, the 3 free books and the surprise gift are mine to keep forever.

183 BPA A2P5

Name	(PLEASE PRINT)	
Address	Apt. No.	
City	State	Zip

This offer is limited to one order per household and not valid to current subscribers.
*Terms and prices are subject to change without notice. Sales tax applicable in N.Y.
All orders subject to approval.

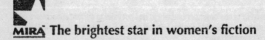

National Bestselling Author

JoAnn Ross

Welcomes you to Raintree, Georgia—
steamy capital of sin, scandal and murder.

Southern Comforts

Chelsea Cassidy is the official biographer of
Roxanne Scarbrough—the Southern Queen of good
taste who's built an empire around the how-to's of
gracious living. It's clear to Chelsea that somebody
wants her employer dead.

As Chelsea explores the dark secrets of Roxanne's
life, the search leads Chelsea into the arms of
Cash Beaudine. And now her investigating becomes
personal with potentially fatal consequences.

Available this September wherever books are sold.

 MIRA The brightest star in women's fiction

MJRSC

A woman with a shocking secret.
A man without a past.
Together, their love could be nothing less than

Scandalous

The latest romantic adventure from

CANDACE CAMP

When a stranger suffering a loss of memory lands on Priscilla Hamilton's doorstep, her carefully guarded secret is threatened. Always a model of propriety, she knows that no one would believe the deep, dark desire that burns inside her at this stranger's touch.

As scandal and intrigue slowly close in on the lovers, will their attraction be strong enough to survive?

Find out this September at your favorite retail outlet.

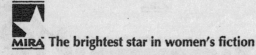

Pick up these fabulous stories by

LINDA LAEL MILLER

Order now to receive these romantic tales
by one of MIRA's most successful authors:

#66014	STATE SECRETS	$4.99 U.S. ☐
		$5.50 CAN. ☐
#66037	USED-TO-BE LOVERS	$4.99 U.S. ☐
		$5.50 CAN. ☐
#66055	JUST KATE	$4.99 U.S. ☐
		$5.50 CAN. ☐
#66073	ONLY FOREVER	$4.99 U.S. ☐
		$5.50 CAN. ☐
#66098	DARING MOVES	$5.50 U.S. ☐
		$5.99 CAN. ☐

(limited quantities available on certain titles)

TOTAL AMOUNT	$
POSTAGE & HANDLING	$
($1.00 for one book, 50¢ for each additional)	
APPLICABLE TAXES*	$_____
TOTAL PAYABLE	$_____
(check or money order—please do not send cash)	

To order, send the completed form, along with a check or money order for the total above, payable to MIRA Books, to: **In the U.S.:** 3010 Walden Avenue, P.O. Box 9077, Buffalo, NY 14269-9077; **In Canada:** P.O. Box 636, Fort Erie, Ontario, L2A 5X3.

Name:_____

Address: _____ City: _____

State/Prov.: _____ Zip/Postal Code: _____

*New York residents remit applicable sales taxes.
Canadian residents remit applicable GST and provincial taxes.   MLLMBL6

MIRA

Look us up on-line at: http://www.romance.net